"I am beyond speechless . . . fantastic storytelling."

—*Lives & Breathes Books*

"I loved this book. . . . Mummert put a lot of depth and soul into her characters."

—*Contagious Reads*

"This is one of those books that will stay with you. The characters are so real that they set up residence in your heart and they will live there for the rest of your life. . . . My heart ached for more."

—*Selena-Lost-in-Thought*

"Dark, edgy, emotional . . . I didn't want it to end!"

—*Belle's Book Blog*

"Wow. LOVE doesn't even begin to describe my feelings for this book. I instantly fell in love with Cass."

—*KTReads*

"*White Trash Beautiful* is the first book I have read by Teresa Mummert, but it is definitely not my last! I loved every minute of it even though parts of it broke my heart. . . . Just writing this review makes me want to read the book again."

—*Smardy Pants Book Blog*

Also by Teresa Mummert

White Trash Beautiful

WHITE TRASH

Damaged

Teresa Mummert

GALLERY BOOKS

New York   London   Toronto   Sydney   New Delhi

G

Gallery Books
A Division of Simon & Schuster, Inc.
1230 Avenue of the Americas
New York, NY 10020

First Gallery Books trade paperback edition October 2013

GALLERY BOOKS and colophon are registered trademarks of Simon & Schuster, Inc.

For information about special discounts for bulk purchases, please contact Simon & Schuster Special Sales at 1-866-506-1949 or business@simonandschuster.com.

The Simon & Schuster Speakers Bureau can bring authors to your live event. For more information or to book an event contact the Simon & Schuster Speakers Bureau at 1-866-248-3049 or visit our website at www.simonspeakers.com.

Interior design by Davina Mock-Maniscalco

Manufactured in the United States of America

10   9   8   7   6   5   4   3   2

Library of Congress Cataloging-in-Publication Data is available.

ISBN 978-1-4767-3208-4
ISBN 978-1-4767-3210-7 (ebook)

This book is dedicated to my amazing husband,
Joshua Mummert.
Not only did he take over the house while I spent hours
on my laptop but he also listened to me ramble on endlessly
about my story. If it wasn't for his continuous support,
I would never have started writing. Every time I've wanted
to give up he has talked me down from the ledge.
I appreciate him more than I could ever put into words.
Thank you for everything.
You are an amazing husband, father, and friend.

WHITE TRASH
Damaged

Prologue

*I*F SOMEONE ASKED me a few months ago if I would ever make it out of the trailer park alive, I would have smiled and told them the lie I told myself every day: I will make it out and have a better life for myself. I don't know if I ever honestly believed it, but it was the one thing that kept me from breaking down and giving up on life. Physically, I've left the trailer park and all of the things that were slowly killing me. But it is all still with me.

I stared off at the charred remains of my past. The ground was scorched and dead. All of my memories and the horrors that went on inside those four walls eviscerated with a tiny flame that flickered inside of my heart for Tucker.

It was time to rebuild my life from the ground up, starting from those burnt remnants. I had to move on from the death of my mother and my unborn child. I had to forgive Jackson for taking everything from me. In truth, I may have never been able to escape had he not destroyed everything I was holding on to. I would never understand why he did the things he did, and maybe I wasn't meant to. But regardless of all that, I could no longer live in the past. I needed to move forward and become the person I wanted to be.

CHAPTER

One

I TOOK A FEW tentative steps through the aftermath of my former life. It hadn't rained since the fire and the ashes coated everything, making it difficult to know where to step. The cheap metal frame lay twisted and charred. The concrete front steps remained, blackened and leading to nowhere. This was the spot I had last seen my father. I continued farther into the debris, refusing to dwell on the person I had lost due to him not wanting to be in my life. *At least Jax* . . . I couldn't even finish my thought. It turned my stomach to think about him as anything more than the animal he was. Fragments of our old boxed television crunched under my foot, and I knew I was facing what used to be the hallway. My throat began to close as I struggled to face my past and walk down this path one last time. It's funny how the memories can hold you hostage on something that no longer existed. I took a deep breath, the air smelling like a campfire, and tilted my face toward the sky. The sun shined down, warming my skin, and the birds called to one another in the distance. There was no yelling, no hate, just life continuing on in the wake of unspeakable tragedy.

I GAZED AT THE BACK of the old trailer next door as I began to walk toward it. My body reflexively sidestepped the old bucket that used to catch rainwater, even though the bucket was long gone and melted into the dirt. I stopped, glancing to my left at my room. A small smile played on my lips as tears began to blur my vision. This was my tiny corner of the world, and for years it felt more like a prison cell. My eyes danced around the neighborhood, taking in all of the life and families that had surrounded me for years, but had been closed off to me by those walls. I kicked at a plank of wood with the toe of my shoe and raised my chin in silent defiance to all that I had been put through inside that prison. It was now that I finally realized that this place was nothing more than a shell. The real confinement was inside of my head. I had been so beaten down mentally that I had convinced myself I couldn't leave, but it was fear that kept me, not these weak walls.

I stepped across what would have been my bathroom. Not all of the contents had disintegrated into nothingness, and I took a moment to take in what remained from all of those years. The pain, the sadness, and the loved ones brutally taken from me burned down to an old flimsy rubber hose and memories that would haunt me for a lifetime. I looked toward my old self's old room and knew that this place didn't hold any good memories. The memories I truly treasured were in my heart, and nothing could take those away from me.

I LET OUT A LONG, deep breath as I heard the tires on the stone parking lot behind me. I glanced over my shoulder, squinting in the sunlight as I looked at the sleek, black Cadillac parked a few feet away from Aggie's Diner. It was time to finally close out this chapter of my life. I had learned and grown a great deal over the last few months, and I was ready to start over completely. No more running and hiding under secrets. I looked back one last time at the place where my trailer had sat before I made my way across the parking lot and slipped inside the open back door of the car. The driver nodded at me once before he got back inside and pulled out of the dusty lot.

It was impossible to block out the voices of those who had once been my entire world. I could still hear Jax apologizing. I could still see the vacant look in my mother's eyes as she slipped into a drug-addled oblivion. The events of the day that would forever change my life replayed on a loop inside of my head as we made our way across town.

I squeezed my eyes closed and rested my head against the back of the seat. I pushed aside the guilt as I tried to focus on the happier moments that had brought my life to this point. The memories that I held sacred in my heart didn't belong to Jax. They belonged to Tucker. He was the reason I could see past those walls.

I SMILED and let my eyes flutter open. Glancing out of the dark, tinted windows I knew we were getting closer. I sat up straight and ran my hands through my messy blond hair.

"Big day," the driver said in a gravelly voice. My eyes focused on his peppered dark hair. He was at least twenty years older than I was. For a brief moment, I wondered if my father's hair would be turning gray or if he had any at all. I shook the memory of him from my head and cleared my throat.

"Very," I replied as we made our way into the city. I began to hum along to the song on the radio as we turned toward City Market.

When I ran away from my problems the first time, I had done it all wrong. I thought all I wanted was to escape from my shitty life and my abusive boyfriend. . . . I never expected to fall deeply, madly in love with someone else. But I also never expected to lose myself in the process and get absorbed into someone else's larger-than-life world that didn't really have a place for me in it.

I stepped out of the car, lost in my own thoughts as I glanced up at the apartment building I had been calling home.

The driver nodded at me with a smile and I returned it, hoping I could keep my nerves at bay for a little longer.

"Thank you," I called over my shoulder as I made my way to the front door and sighed before pulling it open and ascending the stairs.

Everything was going to change once again. I pulled open my apartment door and scanned the living room that was filled with cardboard boxes containing what little I had accumulated in the few months that I had lived on my own.

I ran my hand over one of the boxes as a light tapping came from the door behind me. I turned to look as it squeaked open and Tucker stood in the doorway.

"Coconut?" He laughed as he ran his hand through his hair and kicked the door closed behind him. I could feel my face turn pink with embarrassment.

"It reminds me of you." I captured my bottom lip between my teeth and chewed on it nervously.

Tucker took two quick steps, closing the space between us, and cupped my face in his hands.

"If you wanted to smell me, Cass, all you had to do was invite me over." His lips pulled into a slight grin. I placed my hand on his as he gently caressed my cheek.

"I did. You were late." I smirked as his eyes met mine.

"My flight was delayed. I'm sorry." His eyes drifted over the stack of boxes behind me. "Let me make it up to you." His gaze flicked from my eyes to my mouth. His tongue rolled over his bottom lip, and I knew I was powerless to resist him any longer. His lips met mine hard, and my knees immediately buckled under his touch. His left arm looped around my back and held me firmly against him, keeping me from falling. Even without hitting the ground, I had fallen for this man a long time ago.

I let my mouth open slightly, and Tucker ran his tongue over my lips, causing me to moan as I pushed my tongue against his. My hands slid up his toned chest and into his messy hair. I gripped it, tugging gently as he deepened our kiss.

Panic began to set in as I thought of where this had gotten us before. My body stiffened involuntarily at the memory. Tucker broke away from our kiss and searched my eyes with worry marring his beautiful face.

"What's wrong?" he asked, struggling to steady his breathing.

"I'm sorry. I don't think I can . . . not yet."

His hand slid from my cheek to the back of my head as he pulled me against his chest.

"I'll wait forever. Just don't run away from me again." He kissed the top of my head. "As long as it takes."

I nodded and listened to the soothing steady rhythm of his heartbeat. I don't know how I ever went a day without hearing the sound of it. His voice broke through my thoughts as his chest vibrated against my ear with each word.

"You ready to go start our forever?"

I pulled back to look up into his eyes. I wanted him to see that I meant every word I was about to say.

"I don't ever want to spend another minute apart." I spoke with as much confidence as I could muster, even though I was terrified about taking this next step with Tuck and leaving my new apartment—my flimsy attempt at a fresh start—behind to spend the next few months on the road with him and his band, Damaged. I glanced around my cramped apartment, suddenly realizing that, even though it was familiar, it no longer felt like my home. Tucker's arms were my home, no matter where they took me.

CHAPTER

Two

I TOOK A DEEP breath and nodded. He tucked a strand of my dirty blond hair behind my ear and winked before turning around and opening the door. Two large men stepped inside and began grabbing boxes to carry out of the apartment. I picked up my small bag that I had packed for our trip.

"Come on." He bent down, grabbing my bag from me and taking my hand to pull me toward the front door. We made our way down the flight of steps and out the door. Tucker's bike was just off the sidewalk. He grabbed my helmet and held it out for me with a smile, revealing his dimples. There was no other place I wanted to be than wherever Tucker was. I watched him straddle his bike and kick back the kickstand. The bike roared to life underneath him as I flung my leg across it and wrapped my arms around Tucker's waist. I had no idea where we were going, and I didn't care. I took my bag from him and looped it over my shoulder. I rested my head against his back and closed my eyes, letting the sunshine beat down on my face as we made our way out of the city.

We weaved through the traffic on I-95 as the larger buildings faded into the distance until we were surrounded by trees. I realized that we were heading toward Eddington. We exited the highway and came to a stop sign. Tucker's hands went to mine and rubbed them soothingly.

"I want to show you something," he called over his shoulder. I nodded against his back as his muscles flexed and pulled as the bike turned down Maple Street. We flew by the roads leading to my old house. I relaxed a little more knowing I wouldn't have to face the demons of my past. We slowed and turned onto an old dirt road lined by trees. As we came through a clearing, I realized where we were. Old Basin Cemetery. Tucker pulled off into the grass and shut off the motorcycle.

"Why are we here?" This wasn't the place my mother and Jax had been buried. I didn't know anyone who had been laid to rest here. I slid off the bike and pulled the helmet from my head, running my free hand through my hair. I looked out over the field that was dotted with headstones: some old, some new. Tucker got off the bike and grabbed my helmet from my hand before removing his. He slid the bag off my shoulder and hung it on the handlebars.

"I have a surprise for you." He reached for my hand and I

let him intertwine our fingers. He pulled me toward the small field, and I let my feet drag, wondering what he could possibly have in store for me.

We leisurely strolled to the back of the cemetery to a small tree with a tiny angel statue placed beside it. I looked up at Tucker with confusion. He let go of my hand and nodded toward the stone. He rubbed his palms together nervously as I stepped forward, tucking my hair behind my ears and bending down to read the inscription.

> Another angel has taken flight
> Cass Daniels & Tucker White

I reached out and ran my fingers over the cold stone, feeling the indents of each letter. Tucker knelt at my side, his hands fisted together in front of his mouth.

"How?" I could barely choke out the word.

"I thought it would be good to have a place to grieve. Somewhere without all of the bad memories." His eyes misted over as he stared ahead at the stone.

It made it all seem so real. My hand fell to my stomach as I thought about that awful night.

"I'm sorry. I just thought . . ." he tried to explain. I reached over and gripped his forearm tightly.

"No, it's perfect. Our child deserved a place in this world." I nodded. He swallowed and looked down at the grass. The wind began to blow, whipping my hair in front of my face. Tucker turned to me and brushed it aside. His forehead fell against mine, and I closed my eyes, breathing in deeply and taking in his scent of freedom. "Thank you," I whispered. He stood and held his hand down to me. I placed mine against his palm, and he effortlessly pulled me to my feet and into his arms.

"Whatever happens with us, we will get through it together. If it hurts you, it hurts me too, Cass."

I nodded into his chest, unable to find the words to express how grateful I was that he fought so hard to be with me.

"Come on. We have memories to make." He pulled back and shot me a wink that still had the power to make me blush. I grabbed his hand as we made the walk back to his bike. No matter how hard I tried to fight it, Tucker and I belonged together. Now we had our own angel looking over us. As we reached the bike, Tucker grabbed my helmet and slid it over my head, fastening the strap below my chin.

"We have a long ride ahead of us." He gripped the waist of my sundress and pulled me closer, kissing me hard on the lips before taking a step back and slipping on his helmet. He got on his bike, and I followed suit, wrapping my arms around his waist and running my fingers along the ridges of his stomach muscles.

We drove out of the small cemetery and headed back onto the highway. I was thankful it was a warm day since I had decided to wear a dress today. Still, the wind made it chilly as we left Eddington and all of our horrible experiences behind us. I had no idea where we were going, and I didn't really care. I watched the cars around us go by in a blur as we made our way to Interstate 75. We rode for hours, only stopping to refuel and stretch our legs.

Traffic began to pick up, and we slowed to a crawl as we made our way to Atlanta. I had never been there before and couldn't wrap my head around the sheer amount of people that populated the city. Everyone had their own destination, and they were oblivious to the hordes of people around them.

Tucker took an exit off the highway and wove his way through the city streets. Everything seemed bigger than life. We pulled up to a stoplight, and Tucker glanced back over his shoulder at me, rubbing my hands that still gripped his waist.

"Hungry?"

"Absolutely," I yelled over the sound of the engine.

He nodded and took off as the light changed to green. After a few more lights and several turns we pulled up at a restaurant that was tucked away at the base of a larger building. It looked like a hole in the wall. I got off the bike, stretching my legs in the most ladylike fashion manageable. I held out my helmet for Tucker and ran my hands through my hair a few times.

"You look beautiful." His grin melted my heart, and I looped my fingers in his as I let him pull me into the small eatery.

I had to do a double take as we entered. The restaurant

stretched far back into the building and was much larger than it appeared from outside. The walls were painted a deep gold with patches of gold leaf brushed right onto the walls. The lighting was so low it was nearly dark, with candles lit at each table. Artwork lined the walls, and I would have thought we were at a gallery had it not been for the tables. A woman in a crisp white button-down shirt and black slacks greeted us as we entered. We followed her toward the back of the room and passed a bar that lined the left wall. There was a set of steps that led down below the main level and held a larger dining area. I suddenly felt extremely underdressed for such a place.

"This is beautiful," I whispered as Tucker looped his arm over my shoulders and pulled me into his side. He gave me a quick kiss on the top of my head. The hostess had stopped at a table and waited for us to take our seats. Tucker pulled out my chair, and I slid into it and waited for him to join me. Instead of sitting across from me, he chose the chair to my left and held my hand as we waited for the waitress to bring us our menus.

"This is . . . more than what I expected." I felt so out of place. Luckily, we had arrived just after the dinner crowd, and being that it was a weekday, we pretty much had the restaurant to ourselves. There was one other couple on the far side of the room. They were older and dressed to the nines. I wondered if they were celebrating an anniversary or something.

Our waitress arrived with glasses of ice water and handed us our menus. She was beautiful. Her hair was more blond than mine, her eyes a sparkling light blue. I watched as she smiled, blushing slightly in Tucker's direction. He smiled back politely, but gave my hand a gentle squeeze under the table.

"I'll have a beer. Whatever you have is fine."

She turned her attention to me.

"I'll have whatever he is having," I said, clearing my throat. These were the girls who worried me. The ones I could see on Tucker's arm, winking at the paparazzi and looking glamorous while his star continued to rise. As the waitress left to grab our drinks, I glanced down at my sundress, tugging at the hem. I wished I had changed into something a bit . . . classier before the trip.

"You look amazing."

I felt my cheeks flush under his gaze. He made me feel like I truly did look amazing. There was an honesty in his voice that I had never heard from anyone else before. I reached for my glass of water and took a small sip.

"Thank you."

His thumb brushed over the back of my hand as I flipped open my menu and tried to concentrate on finding something to eat. The confusion I felt as I was trying to decipher the Italian menu must have shown on my face because Tucker laughed at me and flipped my menu closed.

"I have no idea what any of it means either. Let's just order a bunch of appetizers. One of them is bound to be good."

I smiled back at him and nodded. I had a tendency to get

overwhelmed. Tucker took everything in stride. I admired that about him.

"So . . . where are we headed?" I asked excitedly. This was the farthest away from home that I had been.

"We have a concert in a few hours at Philips Arena. It's kind of a big show. We are headlining for a new band. Probably the biggest concert we have had yet." He grinned and for once he looked nervous. I gave his hand a reassuring squeeze.

"Shouldn't you be rehearsing?" I felt guilty that once again his band was sitting around waiting for him because of me.

"They understand. Trust me. It was Terry's idea for me to come find you."

I thought back to the Twisted Twins. Neither gave off the "love conquers all" vibe. In fact, had they not defended my honor when I worked at the diner, I would have been frightened of them.

The waitress returned with two Budweiser bottles and glasses. Tucker waved the glasses away and picked up his bottle, taking a long swig.

"They may be okay with it now, but how much longer are they going to be okay having to change their schedules to accommodate me?" I grabbed my bottle and took a small sip.

"You're not planning on leaving me again, are you?" He cocked his eyebrow up as his eyes scanned my face.

"Of course not."

"Then there's nothing to worry about." He shrugged and

took another sip. The waitress returned from disposing of the unused glasses. She held a pen and pad in her hands, waiting to take our order.

"Have you decided?" she asked, her eyes flicking to me but then resting intently on Tucker.

"We'd like one of each of your apps." He smiled, grabbing my menu and placing it on top of his and holding them out for her to take. I did not miss the fact that she went out of her way to touch his hand with her fingers as she grabbed the menus from his hand.

He gave me a small grin, noting my jealousy.

"So . . ." He cleared his throat and took another drink. "What have you been up to while I was on the first leg of the tour?"

I picked at the label of my beer.

"Working mostly. But hey, I saw that you will be doing an awards show soon? That's actually really exciting!" I wanted to add that I had heard about the actress he had been linked to and was dying for him to tell me that there was no truth to the rumors, but I knew I couldn't ask . . . and I knew he wouldn't bring it up. After all, I had been the one who left him, and he had no obligation to be faithful to an absentee girlfriend. Although it's not like he had any reason to worry about what I'd been up to. I couldn't look at another man after being with Tucker. He had ruined me for anyone in the future.

"What about you?"

He took another long pull from the bottle, emptying it. He sat it on the edge of the table and nodded toward the waitress who quickly came and cleared it as she went off to fetch him another beer. I watched her leave, wondering if I could handle what he was going to say. Tucker had been nothing but kind to me, always honest and faithful and passionate when we were together, but I would be lying to myself if I said I knew him inside and out. Even today, I had seen new sides to him that I hadn't known existed. I didn't know if those sides had grown from what we had been through together, or if they had been there all along, bubbling under the surface.

"I spent most of my time writing, practicing with the guys. They would drag me out whenever they could, trying to get me to cheer up."

Those words sat on my chest like a ton of bricks. As I watched the waitress return with Tucker's drink, she smiled, and he returned it politely. I took a deep breath. I had to stop letting jealousy get the best of me. Tucker and I were together now, and that was what mattered. I needed to erase those months of separation from my mind and focus on our future— we both deserved, and clearly needed, a clean slate. And there was no place for jealousy in our future together. Easier said than done when you're dating a rock star.

CHAPTER

Three

AS WE MUNCHED on our appetizers, Tucker's eyes lit up as he filled me in on what had been going on with the band. A lot had changed for them since they landed the music awards gig, and they were playing bigger venues and getting invited to join fairly established bands in concert. But the most exciting news, which he could hardly deliver without beaming, was that Damaged was going to be making their debut music video for Loved.

"That's surreal." I was incredibly proud of all that Damaged had accomplished in only a few months' time.

"It's a really big honor to have Jeff Jones direct. He's done videos for all of my favorite bands. We only have a couple of months to come up with the concept and how we want the band portrayed." Tucker was beaming, and his excitement was contagious.

"You're going to do great." I smiled, loving the way his eyes lit up as he spoke.

"You'll be right by my side." He winked, and the realization of how much everything was about to change hit me. A few months ago I was worried where my next meal would be coming from; now I had to find something to wear on a music video shoot.

We finished our food and made our way out to the motorcycle so we could meet up with the rest of the band. I could feel my nerves tying knots in my stomach as we approached the arena. I hoped the rest of Damaged didn't harbor any bad feelings for me, but I wouldn't blame them if they did.

As we pulled into the parking lot of the Philips Arena, it finally hit me how different things had really become. The parking lot overflowed with cars, and throngs of people lined the sidewalks . . . all waiting to see Tucker play. We rode around to the back of the oversized building and parked next to Damaged's tour bus. The bus was dark, and I was thankful I wouldn't have to come face-to-face with the other members just yet.

Tucker took my hand and led me up onto the bus.

"I just want to change my shirt. It will only take a second."

I nodded at him and followed up the short set of steps. The bus couldn't even be called a bus—it was practically a house on wheels. There was a large table with a bench seat that covered three sides. A mini kitchen sat directly across from the table.

Next to that was a narrow hallway that appeared to be lined with bunk beds of sorts. I couldn't see what was past that. It was more than obvious a bunch of young guys with no supervision lived here. My shoes stuck to the floor, and soda bottles overflowed from the tiny trash can by the table. The bus smelled like a mixture of cheap cologne and alcohol.

Tucker released my hand and gave me a quick kiss on the cheek.

"I'm going to go change." He walked down the narrow hall and disappeared into a door at the back of the bus.

"Hand me a water," a voice called from behind one of the curtained beds. I jumped at the sound, not knowing who it was or who they were talking to. He was silent for a minute, and I held my breath, trying not to make a sound. "Please?" He sounded sad, almost in pain. I turned behind me and scanned the kitchen area for a fridge. I located a mini fridge under one of the cabinets. I pulled it open and found a bottle of water. I slid my hand behind the curtain. Warm fingers circled mine as he took the drink.

"Thank you," he said, still not revealing his identity.

"You're welcome," I replied, not wanting to be rude.

"You groupies are good for *two* things," he said and laughed to himself. Suddenly, the curtain pushed open and I was face-to-face with a nearly naked man. His hair was cut short, not very rock star. His body was thick but muscular and I couldn't see any tattoos.

"Excuse me?" I took a step back, suddenly feeling like the space was closing in on me.

"Cass?" He jumped down from the top bunk, filling the little space between us with his large, muscular body that was only covered by a pair of black boxer briefs. "Didn't think I'd see *you* again."

I shook my head as the drummer for Damaged held out his hand for me to shake.

"Eric."

I took his hand and shook it as Tucker made his way out of the room in the back of the bus. He was wearing a vintage-wash, dark blue T-shirt that read #Damaged and a pair of dark, tattered jeans.

"Hey, E." Tucker nodded his head toward Eric as he slipped behind me, resting his hands on my hips. "How's the headache?"

"I'll live. You coming to practice?" His eyes went from Tucker's to mine as he ran his hand over his buzzed hair. I hoped he wasn't worried that I would be responsible for Tucker missing any more practices or gigs.

"Yeah, I'm coming. Throw some clothes on. Let's go find the twins."

Tucker guided me toward the steps to leave. I glanced over my shoulder at Eric whose eyes were already on mine, and he had a smirk on his face. He certainly wasn't shy.

We stepped down off the bus and Tucker spun me to face

him, pushing my back against the bus, his body pressed hard against mine.

"I can't wait to have you in my arms like this every night." His lips pressed against mine. I let my arms loop around his neck and pulled him closer, not wanting any space between us. Eric stepped down out of the bus and cleared his throat. Tucker pulled back and playfully hit him on the arm, but it was more than apparent that these guys weren't the best of friends.

"Where are Chris and Terry?" he asked E as his fingers laced in mine and I was being pulled behind them as we made our way to the back entrance of the large building.

"Should be inside. Lizzy is with them." He shot a look to Tucker who shook his head and smiled. I wanted to ask who Lizzy was, but I knew I would find out soon enough. We slipped past a giant beast of a guard and made our way down a maze of hallways. After a few turns that left me feeling like we should be right back where we started, we found the rest of the band.

The twins sat with guitars in hand as they played a tune that I didn't recognize. A girl with a mass of dark curly hair sat with her arms laced around one of the twins, her head resting on his shoulder. As Tucker closed the door behind us, everyone's eyes landed on us.

"Hey, Cass!" the twin with the girl attached to him called out.

"Hey," I called back with a wave.

"Hey, Terry, groupies aren't allowed back for practice," Eric teased from behind me. Terry threw his guitar pick at him, and we all ducked as it flew by.

"Cass, this is Lizzy. Lizzy, Tucker's girl, Cass," Terry said to the girl who had resumed her position at Terry's side.

We both nodded and smiled at each other.

"How was the ride?" Chris asked as he continued to mind-lessly strum his guitar.

"It was long. I don't think I'll ever be able to walk right again," I joked.

"That's what she said," the twins called out in unison. The room erupted with laughter. I didn't quite get the joke.

"Let's get some work done," Tucker called out over the laughter. Lizzy reluctantly peeled herself from Terry's side, and he playfully smacked her on the ass as she pushed off the couch. She turned around to glare at him, and Terry just smiled.

"What? You fucking like it."

She shook her head in disapproval, but the reddening of her cheeks revealed she liked it more than she let on. Tucker kissed me on the forehead and went to join the others on the couches.

"Come on," Lizzy said as she looped her arm in mine. "Let's go check this place out."

I gave her a small smile and let her drag me away. I needed to give Tucker some time to get ready, and I had to admit, I was curious about Lizzy. She was wearing a plaid shirt tied above her navel and short jean shorts paired with brown worn-out cowboy boots. Not the typical attire for a Damaged concert. I liked her already.

We left the room and made our way into a giant open area lined with tables full of merchandise and some snacks. She grabbed a small bag of chips and held it up to me. I shook my head, and she made a face and sat it back down on the table, looking for something more appetizing.

"So, you're a local." She wasn't asking. I just nodded as we walked the length of the table, around a group of guys who looked like they belonged in a band. Maybe they did, but I didn't recognize them, not that I knew what any of these people looked like.

"You're not?" I had no idea where Lizzy came from or how she ended up wrapped in Terry's arms. I was curious.

"I'm from Ohio. I traveled with some friends to a Damaged concert in Pennsylvania."

"Oh," I said and took an apple from her hand that she was holding out for me. Her green eyes glowed against the fluorescent lights of the building.

"I'm not a groupie." She looked down at her apple, picking at the sticker on it.

"Of course not," I said, trying to reassure her that I was not judging her. I had been judged enough to know that it doesn't feel good.

"He says he loves me." She tucked her hair behind her ear and gave me a big toothy grin.

"I'd like to hear all about it. How you met and all," I said as we began to walk toward another set of halls.

"I snuck backstage after the concert."

I stopped walking, and she turned around to look at me.

"Does that happen a lot? People sneaking backstage to see the bands?"

"Well, yeah. You gotta do what you gotta do, right?" She smiled again. I began to walk with her, wishing I hadn't asked to hear this story. "So, anyway, I didn't have my mind set on anyone in particular. I was willing to take what I could get."

I felt like my lungs would explode if my breathing accelerated any more.

"The girls were rough that night. I mean, you would not believe what some girls see as concert attire. I wouldn't walk around my apartment in those kinds of clothes." She rolled her eyes, and we turned another corner, making our way down another hallway. We could faintly hear the screaming of the crowd on the other side of the wall.

"I worked my way through security and made it to the after-party."

"After-party?" I wasn't sure I wanted to know, but my curiosity was getting the best of me.

"Yeah, there is always an after-party. You will see tonight. It is wild." She giggled and tossed her hair over her shoulder.

"Anyway, I met Terry, and we talked for hours. I mean, he held my hair when I puked. I knew he was a keeper."

Well, if that wasn't love, I didn't know what was. I tried to keep my look of disgust off my face. A loud booming like thunder felt like it was shaking the walls.

"What is that?" I asked, looking up and down the hallway.

"That's Filth. Aren't they amazing?" she asked, her eyes twinkling again. I suddenly worried for Terry and how long this girl was planning to stick around. She seemed nice, but hardly the marrying type. For all I knew Terry had said he loved her just to get a little company. It wasn't my place to pry.

"So . . . how long have you been with Damaged?"

She looked deep in thought as she tried to figure it out.

"Two . . . no . . . three weeks." She looped her arm in mine again and tossed her apple core into a trash can. I hadn't even begun to eat mine, but I had no appetite. I tossed mine in behind hers.

We passed through a set of double doors. On the other side stood a giant, burly man blocking the way.

"Hey, Trig. Can we watch?" She was on a first-name basis with the security? She was good. He smiled and stepped aside so we could see the stage from the left-hand side. The music was bone-rattling loud, but the band sounded amazing. The lead singer was a female, and she definitely held her own.

"What's the story with you and Tuck?" she yelled into my ear. It didn't get by me that she had referred to him as Tuck, as if they went way back. I wondered how well they actually knew each other.

"It's complicated," I yelled back, not taking my eyes off the stage.

"It always is." She laughed and the crowd roared as the song ended and the band began to play again.

We didn't talk through the next few songs. Lizzy screamed and called out the name Derek, and I wondered if she knew him personally like she knew Terry. My mind went back to Tucker. The thought made my stomach twist into horrible knots as I tried my best to push the idea out of my head. Tucker had never given me any reason to think he was like that. Still, I left him, not the other way around. During our time apart, he had been free to do whatever . . . or whomever he wanted. Faced with the reality that women like Lizzy had been—and would continue to be—all too willing to throw themselves at him night after night, I suddenly felt like I was going to be sick.

"You all right?" Lizzy leaned in closer to me, engulfing me in her flowery scent.

"I'm fine."

"You are pale. Let's get you some water." She waved the security guard away, and he stepped to the side to let us back through the double doors. As they closed behind us, the muffling of the band helped immensely.

"I think I just need to cool off." I gave her a weak smile,

grateful that she was concerned, that she seemed to be looking out for me. It was a nice feeling, and a sadly unfamiliar one. Maybe I'd been too quick to judge. If Terry liked her, she couldn't be that bad. We began walking back through the maze of hallways and ended up at the table of snacks.

"How do you know your way around here so well?" I grabbed a bottle of water from the table and drank half of the contents. I felt better instantly.

"I have a really good memory." She laughed.

"Can I ask you a question?"

She cocked her head to the side, waiting for me to ask.

"How do you tell the twins apart?"

She laughed hard, taking the bottle of water from my hand and finishing it off.

"All right. I'll tell you my secret, but you can't tell anyone else. Not even the twins."

I nodded, agreeing not to tell a soul. She leaned in closer so no one would overhear us.

"Terry has a freckle right below his right ear. Once I noticed, it stood out like a sore thumb." She laughed. "There are other things, once you get to know them. Terry is sweet and calm, Chris is more of a wild card, always joking and being loud. Chris wears a giant thumb ring on his left hand with this big old gaudy blue stone in it. He calls it his good luck charm."

I smiled at her as she became more animated as she told me

all of the things she learned about the twins. It dawned on me that if she'd been with Damaged for the past few weeks, I was likely the first female she'd probably had the chance to talk to for a while; she hadn't mentioned any other groupies who had joined the tour. It must be exhausting putting up with these guys day and night. I'd imagined Dorris, the band's manager and Tucker's adopted mother, was not any kind of friendly comfort. I suddenly wondered where she was.

"What about the rest of the guys?"

"Umm . . . well, E is very intense. He parties hard but never really looks happy, ya know? He's a closed book."

". . . and Tucker?" I braced myself for her answer.

"You know Tucker." She laughed and playfully nudged me.

"Yeah," I replied shyly.

Lizzy pushed open the door to our left and we were back where we started. The guys all looked up from their places. They were no longer playing and looked to be in the middle of a heated discussion. The silence was worse than standing next to the stage as Filth played. Tucker stood and came to my side, kissing me on the cheek.

"Having fun?" he asked with a smile.

"Awesome!" I smiled.

"We had a great time. Lots of girl talk," Lizzy chimed in as she bounced her way over to Terry and sat down on his lap.

"Yes, girl talk," I agreed, and gave him a small playful smile.

The door opened and an older man stuck his head in.

"You're on in five, guys." He nodded to the band and closed the door behind him.

Tucker sighed and motioned for the other members.

"Let's go kick some ass." The others stood and made their way to the door. Tucker gave me a kiss on the lips, lingering for a moment.

"I've missed you." His forehead fell against mine, and for a second we were the only ones on the planet.

"I've missed you, too."

Eric pushed by us angrily, and I fell into Tucker who grabbed me in his arms.

"Fuck and get it over with so we can go play this gig." He left the room before either of us could process the words.

"What is his problem?" I pulled back and searched Tucker's eyes.

"He's having a bad day." Tucker winked and kissed me one last time before making his way out of the door.

"Take care of my girl, Lizzy," he called over his shoulder as they made their way down the hall.

Lizzy came to my side, slinging her arm over my shoulder as we watched the guys turn and disappear down another hall.

"What's up with Eric?"

"Like I said, he is intense." She laughed and shook her head. "He and Tucker get under each other's skin a lot. I don't know what it is. Almost like brothers, ya know?"

I nodded. I didn't know what sibling rivalry was like personally, but I got the idea.

"Come on. Let's go watch the guys perform." She tugged, and I followed, eager to see Tucker sing again.

We made our way back down the labyrinth of hallways until we were stage left. The guys stood off to the side, deep in discussion, so we hung back and waited for them to be called to the stage. The twins headed onstage first and the crowd screamed in excitement as they strummed a few notes on their guitars. Next Eric made his way onstage. Losing his shirt in the process and looking like he was headed to a fight. He took his seat behind the drums and slowly began to play a beat, complementing the guitars. Tucker began to sing before he even made his way up the steps. The crowd went insane. I had to cover my ears to keep from going deaf.

I didn't recognize the song, but I did recognize the sadness in Tucker's voice. I clutched the heart necklace he had given to me and squeezed it in my palm, wishing I could run onstage and throw my arms around him. He placed the mic in the stand as he sang about having to say good-bye. His eyes glanced my way as I stood helplessly offstage, forced to listen to him croon about pain that I had caused. Lizzy put her arm around me as she swayed to the music, causing me to sway with her.

I struggled to keep my tears at bay, smiling so he wouldn't see my sadness, but I felt his. We hadn't spoken much about me leaving, about our time apart—it was too hard. But I knew there was still so much left unsaid, so much hurt that time hadn't yet healed. And suddenly it was all hitting me through his soft yet powerful melody. Soon the song ended and faded into the next, an angrier piece about a man scorned. It was like a secret invitation into Tucker's private thoughts, and it was terrifying. I had no idea the pain I had caused him. I was too wrapped up in my own hurt.

"Great song, right?" Lizzy was singing along and bouncing up and down to the beat.

Tucker didn't glance my way, and I was happy that I wouldn't have to see the look in his eyes at that moment. I did notice Eric looking in our direction and wondered what was going on with him and Tucker. I hoped again that I wasn't the cause of any turmoil between the members of the band . . . but I couldn't help but sense that I was. Clearly things between Tucker and me had fueled quite a bit of their recent set list.

Tucker's voice became a distant humming as I let myself sink inside my own thoughts. I needed to block out thoughts like that to keep from running again. I had come all this way and refused to leave him again. I just hoped I was strong enough to keep that promise.

But if the band didn't want me around, how long could I stay, causing tension between them? I couldn't wait for the guys to finish their set so I could have Tucker by my side, but the end of the concert also meant the beginning of the after-party. I could only hope that the images playing through my mind were gross exaggerations: women running around naked, begging to sleep with whomever would take them; drugs passed freely among bandmates and groupies. For the first time in weeks, I missed the trailer park. The predictability. Nothing changed from day to day. I knew what life had in store for me and never had to wonder what tomorrow would bring. Not that it was ever good. But at least I knew.

I glanced over at Lizzy who was consumed by the music, singing along. I wanted to be carefree, enjoy myself without having to wonder what curveball would be thrown my way next. But at that moment Tucker's eyes found mine. I smiled, and he smirked back at me with a half grin that put me at ease.

"He's got it bad," Lizzy yelled into my ear, causing my grin to spread from ear to ear.

I pushed the negative thoughts from my mind and decided to embrace the moment. I shook my hips as we listened to a few more songs. The set ended and Tucker made his way down the steps, wrapping his hands around my waist and lifting me from the ground to kiss me.

"Do you know how hard it is to be on that stage while you're over here shaking your ass like that?" He smiled as he spun me in a circle and placed me back on the ground.

"You signing, man?" Chris asked as the band gathered beside us.

"Yeah, I'm coming," Tucker replied, his eyes glued to mine. "Wait for me," he whispered.

"I'm not going anywhere," I assured him. And I meant it.

Lizzy wrapped her fingers around my arm at the elbow and pulled me back from Tucker's embrace.

"There will be plenty of time for this at the after-party." She laughed, but the look from Tucker made her stop short.

I suddenly wished she had never told me about the parties. Maybe I wasn't invited. Maybe Tucker didn't want me hindering his chances with the adoring fans. I shook the thought from my mind. Tucker wasn't Jax, and he had never given me a reason not to trust him. We were together now. He was my future. . . . I needed to stop letting the baggage I still carried from my past influence my expectations of Tuck.

"Come on, man." Terry was trying to get the band to follow him so they could greet the fans. Tucker kissed my temple and backed up a few steps before turning to follow, running his hand through his hair.

"What was that about?" I turned to Lizzy who was digging through her pockets and pulling out a pack of cigarettes. I pulled in a deep breath at the sight of them. I hadn't thought twice about smoking since I had quit, but seeing them made me crave them all over again.

Lizzy shrugged as she pulled a cigarette from the pack.

"These artist types are so moody." She smiled, but it didn't reach her eyes. "Want one?" She held out the pack to me and I waved them away, but my nerves were killing me.

"Sure, just one won't hurt." I pulled one from the pack and

nodded in thanks as she slid them into the back pocket of her jean shorts.

"Come on." She cocked her head toward an emergency exit door.

"We will be back in five. Don't forget about us," she called to the security guard who was still blocking the door to the hallways. He nodded in our direction.

There was a breeze, but the air was warm, and after being in that giant stadium packed tight with bodies, it felt good. Lizzy dug a lighter out of her front pocket, struggling with the tightness of her clothing. She flicked the lighter and held it out for me. I leaned in, cigarette in mouth, and drew in a long, deep breath. She lit hers and leaned back against the door. Smoke clouded around us as we stared off at the sea of cars.

"So, how did you and Tucker meet?"

I glanced over at Lizzy who was flicking her ashes and tugging at the knot in the front of her shirt.

"He came to a diner I used to work at." It felt a million years in the past but also like I would wake up and be in that shitty trailer. She nodded and didn't say anything. I think she was waiting for me to elaborate, but I didn't even know how to continue that story. I was actually surprised she didn't know it. Maybe Tucker didn't want to think about me while I was gone.

"You in love?" She glanced over at me, judging my reaction to her question.

"Yeah." I didn't hesitate. I didn't need to. No matter how

torn I was about wanting to stay away from Tucker, I knew without a doubt that it was because I loved him.

She smiled and flicked at her cigarette again.

"You love Terry?" I barely knew him, but I still felt like someone should look out for him. Play the protective big sister.

Lizzy shrugged and flicked the butt of her cigarette out onto the blacktop.

"I'm here until he gets tired of me and trades me in for someone else. Come on. The guys are going to be done soon." She winked and looped her arm in mine. I flicked my cigarette and let her drag me through the giant metal door.

CHAPTER

Four

HE AFTER-PARTY WAS in full effect. The back hallway maze was filled with fans. The room that held the snack table was now just a sea of bodies. Alcohol was flowing from every direction, and I gripped Tucker's hand to keep from getting lost in the crowd.

"Stay with Lizzy. I'm going to get us a drink." Tucker spoke loudly into my ear as the guitarist from Filth began strumming a tune. I nodded and smiled over at Lizzy who was making out with Terry and had no idea that I was anywhere near her. I sighed and let go of his hand, the sea of people swallowing him up the moment he took a step away from me. I spotted Eric sitting on the back of a sofa, sipping a bottle of beer. I smiled as his eyes met mine, happy to see a familiar face. I made my way closer to him, wondering why he looked so pissed off.

He nodded his head as I approached, taking another drink.

"Hey," I said lamely as I turned to look over the crowd.

"Hey. Where's Tucker?"

I glanced around but couldn't spot him.

"He went to get us some drinks." I tucked my hair behind my ear as I stood on my toes to see better.

"Hmm . . ."

"What?" I turned. He shook his head and pointed with the neck of his bottle to a table set up along the far wall, lined with drinks of every variety. Tucker was nowhere in sight. I pulled my eyebrows together as I searched again, wondering where he'd gone, feeling an inexplicable sense of jealousy knot in the pit of my stomach.

Suddenly, two arms wrapped around my body, pulling me back into him. The smell of coconut mixed with beer filled the air around me. He held a bottle out in front of my face as he kissed my neck.

"Have you been smoking?" he asked as he turned me around to face him.

"Where were you?" I asked.

"Bathroom down the hall," he replied. I glanced back at the spot on the couch where Eric had been sitting, but it was now empty.

"What's wrong?"

"Nothing." I shook my head, feeling like an idiot. His free hand slid onto my hip bone and pulled my body back against his. I closed my eyes and let my head fall back onto his shoulder. His fingers scrunched the fabric of my dress as his hips slowly began to move with the music from the guitar, grinding into my backside. His breath blew across my neck as his lips hovered dangerously close to my skin. I knew I wasn't ready to take things further with Tucker, but my mind and my body had two very different ways of thinking. I pushed back against him and he hissed between his teeth.

"God, I missed you." His lips finally kissed their way up my neck toward my ear. I swallowed hard, not wanting to push him away. My mind was spinning as his fingers splayed over my stomach, and my body tensed involuntarily as I thought of the baby we'd lost. His lips pulled back from me and his forehead rested against the side of my head as he tried to get his breathing under control.

"I'm sorry." He tightened his grip around my waist and hugged me from behind.

"Don't be. You didn't do anything wrong," I tried to reassure him.

"Get a room." Chris laughed and both of our heads shot up to see him smiling at us.

"Hey, man," Tucker said as he released me and came to stand beside me.

I took a long drink from my beer and tried to calm my emotions.

"Where's Terry?" Tucker asked.

Chris glanced around the room before spotting Lizzy and Terry making out like high schoolers in the corner.

"He's professing his love to his groupie." Chris rolled his eyes and laughed, but he didn't seem very happy.

"She seems nice." I always had to put my two cents in.

"She would fuck him over in a second. I guarantee it." He pushed his dark hair back from his face.

"Maybe you're jealous," Tucker jabbed. Chris exaggerated his shocked expression.

"Of that? Hell no, man. I am not the marrying kind." He winked at me and grinned from ear to ear as he took a drink. "Why pick one when I can have a different one every night?" He gestured to the sea of women around him. I made a gagging sound and rolled my eyes, causing Chris to laugh even harder.

"Maybe you just haven't met the right one," I added, glancing at Tucker and feeling my cheeks blush.

"I am having too much fun with all the wrong ones." He glanced back over his shoulder at his brother before sighing. "I miss my brother, though. I haven't had a moment alone with him since Lizzy showed up." Tucker patted Chris on the shoulder.

"Let's get you another drink." Tucker linked his fingers with mine, and we made our way over to the table that was loaded with alcohol. The guys poured some shots and clinked their glasses together before downing the harsh liquid. I declined on the hard stuff but opted for another beer, feeling my-self finally begin to relax.

It wasn't long before the other band members migrated to us. The guys laughed and drank, stopping to chat with an eager fan. Lizzy joined in and had to lean on Terry to even stay up-right. Tucker kept a hand on me, as if he was afraid that I would vanish. I couldn't blame him, but he didn't need to worry. I didn't want to be anywhere but by his side.

A girl flung herself at Chris, clinging to his side like a baby monkey. He smiled down at her, brushing her hair off her fore-head in an almost sweet gesture.

"Not a chance." He peeled her arms from his waist and turned back to the group to continue drinking.

"You are a pig!" I threw a piece of cut-up cheese at him.

"Groupies don't have feelings." He shot a glare over to Lizzy who sank deeper into Terry's side.

"Don't be a dick." Terry's tone was even and calm, but he was serious.

"It's true." Chris shrugged, grabbing a few pieces of cheese off the table and popping them into his mouth. "I can prove it."

All eyes were on Chris as we waited for his brilliant revela-tion. He continued to eat and poured himself another shot, his eyes glancing up to see us all waiting patiently.

"Not now." He smiled and everyone groaned. "Who wants another shot?" He yelled and all the guys held out their glasses. I watched as Lizzy pulled back from Terry and whispered something in his ear. He nodded and gave her a quick kiss before she headed out through the crowd. I wanted to go after her and make sure she was okay, but it wasn't my place. Besides, I wasn't sure it was possible to break Tucker's death grip on me.

"Hello?" I glanced away from Lizzie's back to see Chris holding out a shot glass overflowing with amber liquid.

"Thanks." I gave him a small smile and took the glass from his hand, smelling it before tipping back my head and letting the alcohol scorch my throat. I slammed the cup on the table and sputtered out a cough, wishing I had something to chase it with.

"Lightweight," E muttered under his breath and held out a bottle of soda for me to take.

"Thanks," I said between swallows. He leaned in close enough that I could smell the mixture of soap and alcohol on him.

"If you want to hang with the band, you need to learn how to handle your liquor. Don't end up like Lezzy." He pointed off in the distance.

"Lizzy," I corrected him. He shrugged and rolled his glazed-over eyes.

"Does it matter?"

What the hell was it with these guys? I could only imagine what they must say behind my back. I was grateful that they didn't do it to my face like poor Lizzy. My heart ached for her.

"Thanks for the tip," I replied.

"That's what she said!" Terry was falling over himself with laughter, sloshing beer from his glass as he struggled to catch his breath.

I rolled my eyes and grabbed my shot glass.

"Another?" I knew in the back of my mind that I didn't need to prove myself to Eric or anyone else, but suddenly I just wanted to fit in, show everyone that I was more than just another groupie.

"Hell, yeah!" Chris poured us all another round. This time when I gulped it down, I kept my poker face on and tried my damnedest not to cry out at the burning pain in my throat.

"Better." Eric gave me an approving look, and Tucker squeezed me closer to his side.

"You okay?" he whispered quietly in my ear, causing the hairs on the back of my neck to stand up. I wondered if my body would ever stop reacting to Tucker that way. I nodded and sat down my glass, wiping my lips with the back of my hand.

"I gotta hit the head. Someone set up the next round," Chris called behind him as he made his way through the crowd toward the bathroom.

I took over filling the glasses, slopping booze everywhere. I heard a few guys behind us greeting the band and turned, finding myself face-to-face with Filth. The five-member band was dressed head to toe in black, their eyes coated in eyeliner. I never would have thought makeup looked good on a man, but it suited them. In the center of the group stood a stunning brunette.

The men shook hands, pulling in to bump shoulders.

"Cass, this is Filth. That's Sarah. . . ." I recognized her as the lead singer, and she inclined her head toward me, her dyed dark hair falling in her face. "That's Poppa, Diggy, Derek, and Matt." He pointed to the other members.

"Nice to meet you. You want a drink?"

"Fuck, yeah!" Derek held out his plastic Solo cup, and the other members followed suit. I filled everyone's glasses, finishing off the bottle of bourbon we had been using. Sarah didn't say a word, but I could feel her eyes on me, judging me. I couldn't help but cower a bit under her gaze as I recalled her powerful presence onstage, the way she commanded the attention of everyone in that stadium with her raw, magnetic confidence. She was intimidating to say the least.

"Cheers," Derek yelled over the noise of the crowd, pushing his chin-length jet-black hair from his face. We all lifted our glasses before drinking them down. This time it went more smoothly, and my body didn't try to reject the harsh drink. Probably not a good sign.

"Where's Chris?" Diggy asked as he handed me his cup for a refill. We all looked at one another for a moment before Terry's eyes widened and he took off, pushing his way through the crowd.

"Oh, shit!" Tucker was on his heels, pulling me behind him.

"What's going on?" I asked as Eric pushed past us, yanking his shirt over his head and trying to catch up to Terry.

"Nothing good." Tucker sighed as we made our way down the narrow hallways. Eric's broad shoulders grew smaller as he began to jog away from us, yelling out to Terry who wasn't responding.

We made our way outside in time to see Terry making his way up the steps of the bus.

"Wait outside," Tucker warned and released my hand as he jogged after the others. I could hear Lizzy scream and then one of the twins was shoved out of the doorway, followed by the other. I put my hands over my mouth as I walked closer. Terry was screaming, nose to nose with Chris who was only wearing a pair of jeans, slung low on his hips like the zipper was undone. The rest of the band tried to work their way between them. As I reached the group, Lizzy stepped into the doorway of the bus, wrapped in a blanket, her hair a wild curly mess as tears streamed down her face.

"You fucked my girl?" Terry sounded more hurt than shocked at his brother's actions.

"She's nobody's girl." His hand gestured to Lizzy. "She's just a groupie!" he yelled, and I saw Lizzy flinch.

"I didn't know. I swear I didn't know!" she cried out between drunken, heaving sobs. "I thought it was you!"

Terry cocked back and swung at his brother, his fist connecting with Chris's temple and sending his body spinning backward until he met the pavement. The other members scrambled to pull Terry back before he could punch his brother again.

Lizzy raced to his side, wrapping her arms around his waist.

Chris rubbed the side of his head, groaning in pain.

"She knew, man. She knew it was me. She isn't any good for you," Chris said angrily, causing Terry to lurch forward again like he was going to finish what he started.

"Don't you fucking talk about her. Don't fucking look at her." Terry looked like a madman as Eric and Tucker struggled to hold him back. "How could you fucking do this?"

"She isn't any good for you," Chris repeated.

I felt helpless watching the band being ripped apart. I felt sorry for Terry. He genuinely cared for Lizzy, and I knew damn well she knew what she was doing . . . who she was doing. What if she went after the other guys? What if she tried to sleep with Tucker? I balled my hands into fists and stalked toward the twins, standing between them.

"He's telling the truth." I glanced over my shoulder at Chris on the ground. I had everyone's complete attention now. I swallowed hard and steadied myself. The alcohol was hitting me full force. "She knows how to tell you guys apart."

"That's not true." Lizzy laughed almost crazily as she shook her head.

"It is. She told me earlier about the freckle . . . the ring that Chris wears." I looked Terry dead in the eye as Tucker and Eric took a step back.

His eyes flicked from me to Lizzy. He pulled her from his body, and she stood, clasping the blanket to her chest.

"You're not gonna believe her are you, baby?" Lizzy's voice took on a sickeningly sweet tone as she placed a hand on his chest. He looped his fingers around her wrist and pushed her hand away.

"Yeah, I am. Get your shit, and get the fuck out." He turned to walk away, off into the darkness.

Tucker stepped forward, wrapped his arms around my waist, and kissed me on the top of the head. Chris pushed himself up off the ground and brushed his clothes off.

"Thanks, Cass," he said as he walked off in the opposite direction of his brother.

"Now this is a fucking party!" Eric yelled drunkenly. That was probably the happiest I had seen him all night. I shook my head against Tucker's chest. He laughed quietly.

"This is going to be an interesting tour."

"Is it always like this?" I asked, gripping his T-shirt in my fingers.

"Sort of." He laughed again, and I pulled back to look at his face. His stormy blue eyes.

"I should have kept my mouth shut." I sighed, glancing over at Eric who was still shirtless and smiling. His eyes danced between Tucker and me. "Are you guys gonna fuck or . . . do you want to go get another drink?"

Tucker looked at me and raised his eyebrow.

"Not a chance." I rolled my eyes and took his hand to lead him back into the building. Eric trailed behind us.

We made our way through the crowd that parted for us to pass, stopping once or twice for Tucker to sign autographs.

We settled in next to the refreshment table, the mood considerably lightened. I made my way to the keg to get us each a drink as Tucker and Eric chatted about songs and the next stop on the tour. Apparently, we were headed to Tennessee for a concert tomorrow. I handed the guys their cups as Eric gave his drink a funny look before his eyes landed on me.

"That's way too much head."

"That's what she said!" I yelled as Tucker spit out his beer in laughter.

"No, she didn't say that. She would never say that." Eric shook his head and smiled before gulping down his drink. I shrugged, feeling weightless and carefree.

"Fuck," E yelled, dropping his cup and crushing his hands to the sides of his head while his face scrunched up in pain.

"What's wrong?" He looked like he was dying.

"You all right, man? You need me to walk you back?" Tucker put his hand on Eric's shoulder, but he shrugged it off.

"I'm fine," Eric said angrily through gritted teeth and pushed back through the crowd toward the exit.

"What's wrong with him?" I turned to Tucker who looked exhausted.

"Old injury from when he was younger. He gets a lot of bad headaches."

"So why does he seem to take it out on you?" It was painfully obvious there was tension between Tucker and Eric; I just couldn't understand why.

Tucker shrugged and finished off his drink, crushing the plastic cup in his hand and staring off into the crowd.

"I'm tired." He grabbed my hand in his.

"Yeah, okay." I brushed my thumb over the back of his hand as we left the party and headed back toward the tour bus.

The bus was quiet. Only Eric was inside. The twins still hadn't made it back from their cooling off period, and thankfully, Lizzy was long gone as well. Which reminded me of someone else who was missing.

"Where's Dorris?" I asked as I followed Tucker back through the narrow bus.

"She got a room in town. She tries to sleep off the bus as much as possible." He smiled. It still seemed weird that she hadn't come to the show. "That's her bed back there." He motioned to the door in the back of the bus. "This is us." He pointed to the bunk directly across from Eric's but on the bottom. I reached out and pulled back the curtain to reveal a very small, coffin-like bed.

I stood and turned back to him in disbelief.

"How are we both going to fit in there?"

He pressed his body tight against me, his lips hovering over mine. My pulse began to race as his hands traveled down my sides to my hips, holding me firmly against him.

"We will find a way." He smirked.

I wanted to melt into him, to wrap my legs around his waist and feel the weight of him on top of me, but it still just didn't feel right, not after all that had happened. "You know I am not ready." I pushed against his chest to give myself some room to breathe.

"Thank-fucking-god. I do not want to hear Tuck moaning and panting," Eric called from his bunk.

"Hey, Eric. You need something for your headache?" I asked, changing the subject in hopes of easing a little of the tension between the guys.

Eric shoved back the curtain to his bunk and squinted his eyes at the light.

"Yeah, sure. Thanks. My pills are in the cupboard above the sink." He gave a half grin.

I found his prescription bottle from the cupboard and grabbed a fresh water from the fridge.

"You sure that it's safe to take with the alcohol you drank?"

"I'll be fine." Eric took the bottle and pulled his curtain closed. Tucker shrugged and gave me an apologetic smile.

"You ready?" Tucker inclined his head toward the bed. I

nodded. Today had been amazing, and I was excited to see what tomorrow would bring.

I climbed into the cramped space, sliding over until I was against the wall. Tucker followed, wrapping his arms around my waist and pulling me tight against him. It felt good to be by his side and able to snuggle up to someone without fear. I blinked a few times until my eyes began to adjust to the light. There were concert photos and articles taped up overhead. I tried to read them, but my eyelids were far too heavy, and the alcohol made it impossible to see clearly. I slipped into a dreamless sleep.

CHAPTER Five

I AWOKE LONG BEFORE Tucker. He looked so peaceful, and I knew he wasn't going to be feeling well after a long night of drinking. I slid my body over his so I could use the bathroom before any of the boys claimed it. Tucker's eyes stayed closed, but his hands shot up, gripping my hips and pinning my body to his. His hips grinded into mine and he smirked. I playfully smacked him on the chest.

"I was trying not to wake you," I whispered, my lips hovering above his. His eyes slowly opened, his face serious.

"Sleep is overrated. Reality is so much better, sweetheart."

I couldn't help the grin that spread across my face as a blush followed like wildfire across my skin.

"Pretty in pink," he joked as he released my hip with one hand and ran his fingers over my cheek. I leaned into his touch as he set every nerve ending in my body off like fireworks.

"I'm already hungover. You guys trying to make me fucking vomit?" Eric called out from the other set of bunks. I laughed and let my head fall onto Tucker's chest.

"Is he always like this?" I whispered, tracing the ridge of Tucker's pec muscle.

"A dick? Yeah, pretty much." He sighed.

"I'm gonna use the restroom." I pushed away from Tucker's body a few inches, the only space the cramped area would allow. I gave him a quick peck on the lips before sliding over him and into the narrow hallway.

To my surprise, the twins were sitting at the small booth-style table near the front of the bus.

"Good morning," I called out to them as I slipped into the bathroom. I turned on the sink and cupped my hands, gathering some water to splash on my face. I rose to examine myself in the mirror. I looked like I had been hit by a truck, and my stomach didn't feel much better. I finished preparing myself for the morning and made my way to the kitchen area of the bus.

"You guys hungry?" I asked as I squatted down in front of the fridge and examined the contents. The twins groaned in unison, obviously feeling the effects of the alcohol and fighting.

"There's nothing in there." Tucker came up behind me, running his hand over my knotted hair.

"More in here than my fridge at the trailer," I joked, but it was true. I glanced over my shoulder at him and his expression saddened.

"How about we go out for breakfast and we can pick up a few things from the store so we can cook on the bus?" Tucker said as I stood and stretched my legs.

"Sounds good." I glanced around the bus. "My bag?"

Tucker pointed to Dorris's room.

"More room to change in there."

I rocked up onto the balls of my feet and gave him a kiss. I loved how thoughtful he was. He rested his forehead against mine and closed his eyes.

"Love you." I kissed him again and made my way down the hall, sidestepping around Eric who had just slid out of his bunk wearing only his boxers. He grinned as I nearly tripped over my own feet, doing my best to avoid any physical contact. Living on a bus with these guys was going to be harder than I thought. I slipped into Dorris's room and found my bag sitting on her bed. I pulled out my favorite pair of jeans and a navy blue tank top. I scanned the room as I yanked off my dress and fumbled with the clasp of my bra.

There were pictures of the band hung on the walls. I walked closer to get a better look as I pulled on my shirt. They all looked happy and were smiling, except for Eric, who wore a scowl in every shot. I wondered how someone who seemed to have it all could be so angry at the world. I could sense that he was using sarcasm to deflect from something bigger that was bothering him, a tactic I had more experience with than I wanted to admit. I'd spent my life dealing with people like him.

People who used drugs and alcohol to mask the pain, but all it seemed to do was amplify it.

There was a lot of tension between him and Tucker, and I hoped that my presence wasn't part of the reason. I made up my mind that I would find a way to talk to him, to let him know that I had no intentions of causing trouble with the band. I slipped my leg into my jeans, falling back onto the bed as I pulled them the rest of the way on.

There was a knock at the door as I pulled up my zipper and fastened the button.

"Yeah?" I called out as I dug through my bag for a hairbrush.

"You decent?" a deep male voice called from the other side.

"Yup," I called back. The door opened and Chris stepped inside, pulling it closed behind him. I furrowed my brow as I wondered what he could possibly want to talk about in private.

"Thanks for backing me up last night." Half of his mouth pulled up into a grin.

"To be honest, I did it for Terry. He deserves better." I gave him a glare, letting him know what I thought of his actions last night. Chris swallowed hard and nodded.

I rolled my eyes and tucked my brush back inside my bag.

"I'm serious. That groupie's been flirting with all of us from day one. She didn't care about my brother. He was too damn blind to see it." He ran a hand through his long hair. "She was along for the ride, and I let her have one."

"So you fucked the girl your brother loved out of the goodness of your heart?"

Before he could respond, another knock came at the door.

Chris slid the pocket door back, revealing Tucker on the other side. Tucker smirked as he heard my comment.

"Don't do me any fucking favors," Tucker joked as he clapped Chris on the back. They both laughed as if the events of last night never happened. Chris made his way back to the front of the bus.

"You ready to head out?" Tucker asked, cocking his head to the side.

"Ready as I'll ever be." I shot him a smile as I slipped my feet into my brown sandals. He looped his hand in mine and we headed off on our morning adventure.

I nearly fell over as I stepped out of the bus. The sun was shining brightly and we were in the parking lot of a mall. It took me a moment to get my bearings.

"They drove while we slept." Tucker stated the obvious, poking me in the ribs.

"Welcome to life on the road," Eric said as he put on a pair of aviator sunglasses.

I followed behind the group as we made our way inside the mall. All of the guys were wearing T-shirts and jeans, none of them looking like the rock stars that graced the stage for thousands of screaming fans hours ago. The only attention we received was from a few girls shooting flirtatious glances. I couldn't blame them; I was surrounded by some very attractive men. I felt like a queen as they flanked my sides and we walked through the stores. For once, I wasn't getting the looks of pity I had grown so accustomed to from working at Aggie's Diner.

We slipped inside a restaurant tucked between a clothing store and a cell phone shop. We all slid in, one by one, to a half circle–shaped booth in the far back corner.

"Feels like home, don't it, Cass?" Eric spat out like he had a bad taste in his mouth.

"What the fuck?" Tucker pushed from his seat, but I grabbed his arm, keeping him from reaching across the table.

"This place is much nicer than the one I worked at." I tried to keep my voice level.

A waitress was at our side ready to take our drink orders. She was beautiful with expertly placed gold highlights in her hair, and her makeup was flawless.

"Wanna upgrade, Tuck?" E laughed, and Tucker lurched over the table between them. The twins each grabbed one of them and pulled them apart.

"What the fuck is wrong with you?" Tucker's voice echoed throughout the small space. Everyone's eyes were on us. So much for keeping a low profile and eating in peace. I pushed against Tucker so he would slide out. I wanted out of there as quickly as possible. I was embarrassed and hurt. I managed to make it outside before the tears started to fall. Tucker was at my side, wrapping an arm around my waist.

"I can't be the reason you guys fight," I said, shaking my head.

"You're not."

"Then why is he being so awful? Is it . . . is it because I left you?" I stopped and turned toward Tucker. He wiped my tears with the pads of his thumbs.

"No, trust me. It has nothing to do with that. Eric is . . . complicated."

I rolled my eyes at the understatement of the century. Tucker smirked, revealing his dimples.

"We've always had a hard relationship. He had a rough life before he joined the band, but other than that, he doesn't say much. He thinks I am just some privileged kid." Tucker laughed sardonically and looked back toward the restaurant.

"But you're not. Have you talked to him about it?"

Tucker's eyes locked back onto mine. His jaw clenched.

"A little, but it's none of his business." His tone was harsh and it made me lean back from him fractionally. "I'm sorry." He ran a hand roughly through his hair as he blew out a deep breath. My heart went out to him

"I wish I knew more about your past, Tuck," I said quietly, hoping he could feel the genuine concern behind my words as I stepped close enough to feel the heat from his body. He nodded once.

"Not now. . . . One day." He leaned in so our bodies brushed against each other, his arms looping behind me and pushing against the small of my back to nudge me closer still. "Cass, don't take this the wrong way, but I need to be sure you are not going to run from me again."

His distrust stung, but I couldn't blame him. I nodded, curling my body into his chest.

"Come on. Let's go get something to eat by ourselves. The guys can manage one meal without killing each other." Tucker laughed, coaxing a smile from me.

I nodded. "It would be nice to have some alone time." I gave him a kiss on the cheek, pausing to take in the loving look in his eyes.

We walked around the mall until we found a small pizza joint. It was early for pizza, but that was one of the things I loved about Tucker. He lived outside of the box, and I loved that life with him was so carefree.

"Tuck, how did you fill your free time when . . . when we were apart?"

"I wrote songs . . . to make me feel closer to you."

"Yeah, I heard." I sighed, dropping my food on the paper plate. "I'm sorry, Tucker. For everything."

"The songs you heard helped me get over the pain. The songs that reminded me of you, of the good times, I don't play onstage. They are just for me." I could feel his eyes on me. I slowly raised my gaze to meet his. "I'd like to play them for you."

"I'd love that." His hand slid across the table and over mine.

"Tucker, I don't want to be the reason your band isn't getting along." I let my shoulders sag, wondering if there was any way I could make all of this right and still be with him. After the baby, I was actually surprised any of the band members talked to me at all. I remembered how Eric reacted when Tucker first told him last summer that I was pregnant, and I felt a stab of pain and hatred as if he'd just spat those cruel words at me again: "Make it *un*-happen." I shook my head to erase the painful memory from my mind.

"You're not causing any sort of rift, Cass, I promise you. But if it makes you feel any better, I'll talk to the guys." He squeezed my hand reassuringly. "You're my number one priority. If I have to choose, it's you every time, Cass." He smiled, but my heart sank. I didn't want him to have to choose, didn't want to be that person. I wouldn't let him destroy everything he had worked for just to be with me. We had sacrificed enough already.

"Maybe I should talk to them. One-on-one. If I can find out what is bothering them, maybe I can help put their minds at ease. Reassure them that I have no intention of coming between you guys."

Tucker smiled at me, tracing over the bones in my hand with the pad of his finger.

"All right." He picked up his slice and continued to eat. After watching him for a moment, I did the same. It felt good being here with him. It felt normal.

We left the eatery and walked around the mall, hand in hand. We stopped in a few shops and I got some clothing. Mostly jeans and a few tops and a pair of pajamas, since I would be in such close proximity to all of the guys. I had some money saved but not nearly enough to cover it all. Tucker insisted on paying since he was the reason I was even here with him. I didn't want to be a charity case, but I had no other choice if I wanted to stay clothed. We finished our shopping excursion by buying a few toiletries.

We crossed the parking lot back to the bus, and I paused to take in the sight of it now that I had the benefit of daylight. It was black and massive like a double-decker bus, sticking out like a sore thumb amongst the cars. The side had gold and brown swirls that trailed back the length of it. We stopped at the entrance as I looked it over.

"Pretty nice, huh? It's used, but it still has a lot of life left in it."

"It's really great." I smiled over at him. He was beaming from ear to ear.

"We're gonna get a new one once we get signed."

I gave him a quizzical look as I ran my fingers over the gold pattern.

"To a label. A big label."

I wrapped my arms around his waist and hugged him. I loved his drive, his ambition, his faith in Damaged.

"It will happen soon. I can feel it."

He kissed the top of my head, hugging me back with his hands full of shopping bags.

"That's the plan."

The door to the bus opened and Eric stepped out, glaring at us as he lit a cigarette. He propped himself against the van.

"Spending up all of his money already?" Eric asked, staring straight ahead as he took a long drag from his cigarette.

"It's not like that. I needed clothes." I rolled my eyes as Tucker placed his hand on the small of my back and guided me to the stairs.

"If you say so," E mumbled under his breath as Tucker and I stepped inside.

"Why is he like that? So angry all the time?" I followed Tucker to Dorris's room. He placed my bags on her bed and began pulling out the contents. "And where the hell is Dorris?"

Tucker sighed, running his hands through his hair as he sank down onto the bed.

"She is still our manager, but she's just . . . managing from afar right now. After having to deal with Lizzy for a few weeks, she began to distance herself from the band." He paused. "And when she found out I was coming for you . . ." His voice trailed off, and he rested his head in his hands.

"She left because of me?" I could feel the bile rising in my throat.

"No. No. She left because this isn't how she planned on spending her golden years." He laughed sardonically and took my hand in his. We both fell back onto the pile of clothing. "I hope she changes her mind."

I squeezed his hand empathetically. It must be tough to feel so close to your big break and yet suddenly abandoned by the person who was supposed to be your biggest advocate. Suddenly I felt even worse for leaving when I did.

"No, it's okay. Dorris is finding us a new manager, and in the meantime, she is still taking care of us. Just from a distance." His free hand trailed down my jaw, and he ran his thumb over my bottom lip. "Everything is fine."

"Tuck, you wanna work on those songs?" Terry leaned against the door frame. Tucker sighed heavily as he stood from the bed. He held out his hand to help me up.

"Just give me a chance to change." I stood, catching my balance before turning to the bags of clothing.

"Actually," Tucker began, and I turned to face him, new shirt in hand. "We need to work on some of those *other* songs. It will be easier to concentrate if it's just the guys."

I scrunched my eyebrows together and dropped the shirt on the bed next to me. I didn't know what part bothered me more. The fact that he would be working on songs about how much I had hurt him, or that he didn't want me there while he did it.

"We need some new tracks to give to the producers." His fingers slipped through his ruffled hair.

"Yeah, no problem. I'll just hang out here." I gave a small

forced smile. He returned the smile and kissed me lightly on the forehead.

"I'll be back soon." He turned and left the room behind Terry. I sunk back down onto the bed and let myself collapse back onto the bags, pushing out a heavy breath.

I wondered how I was going to spend the next few hours. Suddenly, I felt alone . . . adrift. I realized that I needed to start earning my keep, contributing to the tour in some way if this was going to be my life—*our* life—for the foreseeable future. I decided to head out and get some groceries so at least the fridge would be stocked when the guys returned. If I couldn't win Eric over with words, maybe I could break that wall down with food.

I got up and changed into a new pair of jeans and a baby blue tank top. I couldn't get on board with the "pre-torn" style that seemed very much in vogue; I bought my pants perfectly intact, knowing full well I would wear them long enough for the holes to form naturally. I slipped my feet back into my sandals and tied my hair back into a messy ponytail, tucking back the stray stands behind my ears.

I sighed and made my way out of the bus and down the short flight of stairs. The weather was warm in the direct sun but not as overbearing as Georgia. I took in a deep breath and surveyed my surroundings. Directly across from the mall and across the highway was a local grocery store. Stepping inside the store, I grabbed the circular off the stand as I made my way to aisle one, eyeballing the coupons and trying to remember how much money remained in my bank account.

I made my way up and down the aisles as I daydreamed about Tucker's performance last night. I couldn't imagine how it must feel to pour your heart out on paper and perform it for the world. It was amazing to watch him light up on stage.

"Damaged girl," a voice called from behind me, shaking me from my thoughts. I spun around to see the lead singer of Filth standing in front of me, looking surprisingly normal.

"That's me, I guess."

"I'm Sarah." She grabbed a box of Lucky Charms from the shelf and tossed it in her cart.

"Cass." I smiled as I chewed nervously on my lip.

"I heard about what you did last night with that groupie. Cool move. It is so hard to find people you can trust in this business."

I smiled, grateful that at least someone knew I was looking out for the guys. "I can imagine."

She began to push her cart by me and I followed, scanning the shelves for anything I thought the guys might like.

"Sitting on that bus is gonna get boring." She glanced back over her shoulder at me and I nodded.

"I'll find something to keep myself occupied." I shrugged as I looked at boxes of instant oatmeal and read over the flavors.

"Just keep your distance from the groupies. I know you

probably learned your lesson last night." She laughed. "They will do whatever they can to break up your relationship and take your place."

"I'm not worried about Tucker."

"Good. Trust is important. He's a good guy. Here." She tossed a box of fruit snacks in my cart. "That is the key to Eric's heart." She winked, and I couldn't help but smile genuinely in gratitude.

"You two?"

"No. It's not like that. I mean, he's nice. . . ." Her voice trailed off.

"Ha! Are we talking about the same guy?"

"I know how he seems to everyone else, but . . . I don't know. I've only talked to him a handful of times, but he is sweet, ya know? There's more going on there than he lets on."

"If you say so."

"I mean, I don't let him talk shit. I stand up for myself, and I think he digs that. I put a stop to the 'that's what she said' bullshit real fast."

"What does that even mean?" I laughed as we turned the corner to the next aisle.

"I don't know. It's stupid. You have to be tough when you're stuck around a bunch of guys all the time."

We had reached the school supplies and paper products. Sarah picked up a spiral notebook and examined the cover.

"I need a new book to write in." She considered it quietly

for a moment before tossing it in her cart. "What is it you do, Cass?"

"Huh?" I looked at her, confused.

"Or want to do? You know, what's your jam, what's your identity? Sing? Cook? Rock climb? Cage fight?" She elbowed me, and I laughed. "I know being on the road doesn't really give you the chance to hold down a steady career, but there's gotta be something you love to do besides sit around in that trailer waiting for Tucker all day?"

"I'm not really sure." I grabbed a notebook off the stack, wondering if Tucker would like it. I hadn't really thought about what I wanted to do. . . . All I'd wanted was an escape . . . and to be with Tucker and support him. But I hadn't yet considered my own passions and dreams.

"That's cute. You should get that one. Use it for a diary."

"Oh, I don't keep a diary." I tossed the book back on the stack. Sarah grabbed it.

"You have to get your thoughts out somehow. My head would explode if I didn't write songs or poetry." She smiled as she held it out to me. I hesitated, but I realized it might be nice to get my feelings down on paper at times when Tuck wasn't there to talk to. Music had always been a large part of my life in helping me when I was feeling down. Being able to create that would be a dream come true. I grabbed it and tossed it in the cart along with a pack of pens.

"Couldn't hurt." I shrugged as we continued through the

store. "So . . . what does your family think of you being on the road with all of these guys?"

"We don't talk much." She tucked her hair behind her ear and frowned as she looked over cans of soup. "You think this is healthy?"

"I have no clue." I grabbed a few cans and began to look over the ingredients. "I don't have any family to speak of either."

"A merry band of misfits." She laughed and bumped me with her shoulder. "Let me know if any of the guys give you trouble."

"Sure. Thanks." I was surprised by how kind and easygoing Sarah was. Watching her onstage she gave off the impression that she was larger than life and more than a little intimidating. It was interesting to see how much of that was a mask and not at all who she really was. It made me realize that what you saw on television or read in magazines had little to do with how these people actually lived.

We collected a few more items and spent a good twenty minutes looking through funky hair accessories. Sarah held up a spool of black ribbon that faded into a pale blue.

"Not very rock star." I laughed and she rolled her eyes.

"I meant for you, would make your eye color pop."

"I'm more of a plain-Jane type." I laughed and grabbed a pack of hair ties from the shelf.

"That isn't a type, Cass. That's a tragedy." She grabbed the hair ties from my hand and tossed them back at the rack. "You are too pretty not to show it off to the world."

By the time we had made it back to the buses I felt light, happy, and optimistic. I didn't realize how much I'd been longing to talk to another woman about everything that was going on. I hoped I saw her again soon. Her kindness had caught me off guard. There was more to her than meets the eye, and she seemed to feel the same way about me, although I didn't see it.

CHAPTER

Six

I PUT AWAY ALL of the groceries and stored the extra cans and boxes in Dorris's room. I grabbed my new notebook and stack of pens and sat down at the tiny kitchen table at the front of the bus.

"My thoughts . . ." I mumbled to myself. "Poetry . . ."

I doodled a few hearts and stars on the paper before I began to write.

Love is like a waterfall

I cringed and scribbled out the words. What does that even mean? I started again, thinking of how much I loved Tucker.

Your kindness filled the emptiness of my soul

Great. Now I was the old bucket in the trailer hallway that caught water from the leaky roof. This was harder than I expected. I scribbled out the words, feeling defeated. I didn't have some hidden talent; I was nothing special. The frustration began to spill out of me as I scribbled onto the paper.

> *They don't know how their words have cut me*
> *Bleeding and dying but you can never hurt me*
> *Again. . . .*
> *I refuse to let this break me, my soul is bruised but you can't shake me*
> *If I die alone in bed, wrapped in my thoughts trapped in my head*
> *I will forgive all you have done wrong, with pen to paper and tell my song*
> *Fill these sheets with my pain, and one day I will learn to love again*

I could hear the band laughing and chatting just seconds before the door to the bus opened. I closed my notebook and slid it under my legs, suddenly embarrassed. These guys were real poets; I'd hate for them to think I could try to create anything close to what they did.

"Hey, sweetheart." Tucker placed his hand on the back of my head as he bent down to kiss me on the lips.

"How'd it go?" I asked as I watched the band mill about in the tiny space.

"Productive," Terry called out as he dug through the cabinets. "Food!"

"Holy shit! We've been anti-robbed!" Eric laughed as he grabbed the box of fruit snacks and slid in the seat across from me at the table.

"You did this, Cass?" Chris asked as he pulled a Gatorade from the mini fridge.

"I did," I said, beaming. "And I bumped into Sarah, too, actually. It was fun."

"If that's what you consider a good time, Tucker is not fulfilling your needs," Eric joked, and Tucker smacked him on the arm before nudging me over so he could sit next to me.

"It was! We hung out, gossiped in the cereal aisle." I grinned at Eric who suddenly looked more interested in my shopping spree. Something about his expression made me wonder if he had an interest in her.

"What's this?" Tucker pulled my notebook out from under him.

"Nothing. It's stupid." I reached for the book as Tucker flipped it open and his eyes danced over the page. He let me pull it from his hands as he stared ahead. His expression was unreadable. "I told you it was stupid."

"No. It's . . . beautiful. You're a natural."

"I want to see!" Eric reached across the table, but I pulled the book back before he could grab it.

"Reach across this table again and you will pull back a nub!"

"Damn! She *has* been hanging out with Sarah." Chris laughed as he shoved some crackers in his mouth.

"So what did you guys talk about?" Eric leaned back in his seat, trying to look unconcerned, but it was obvious he was crushing on her.

"A lady never tells." I smirked.

"True. Now spill it."

I narrowed my eyes at Eric as Tucker chuckled. He slid his hand under the table and squeezed my knee as he winked at me, which sent butterflies into flight in my stomach. Sometimes it still didn't seem real that I was dating him.

I leaned my elbows on the table like I was ready to spill all of the juicy details of our chat.

"She said you have a really big . . ."

Eric leaned forward, giving me his undivided attention.

"Ego." I let out a laugh, and Eric threw a fruit snack at my head.

"Fine. Don't tell me." Eric's focus turned to Tucker. "What's in the notebook?"

All of the band was quiet waiting for some big reveal.

"Poetry," Tucker replied as he ran his hand through my hair, slipping it behind my ear.

"I had no idea you were so deep." Terry looked genuinely surprised.

"That's what . . ." I began, and all of the guys burst out in laughter.

"No . . . just, no," Chris said as he shook his head.

"You should write more. You have a real talent, sweetheart." I could have melted under Tucker's gaze.

I shrugged, embarrassed at the attention, especially since it didn't feel warranted.

"We have a meeting with a potential manager in half an hour. We should get ready." Tucker kissed my temple before sliding out of the booth and stretching.

The band scattered as they took care of personal business before the meeting. Tucker smiled as he held out his hand to me. I took it, letting him pull me from the booth. His hand slid to the small of my back, pulling me against him.

"I'm serious about the poetry," he whispered. "You should keep writing."

"Thank you." It was incredibly hard to slip back into the mind-set of who I was back in the trailer park, but it was worth it to hear someone as talented as Tucker tell me I was good at something. I pressed my lips against his and let my eyes fall closed. I loved how his kiss could make us feel like the only people in the world, even in a crowded bus. My lips fell open as Tucker's tongue ran over my bottom lip. We deepened our kiss, and I was breathless by the time I pulled back for air. My eyes slowly opened to see the rest of the band watching us. I was mortified.

"You guys need to get a life." Tucker laughed and shook his head. I wanted to crawl in our bed and hide from the world.

"We need to get a video camera," Eric shot back, and Chris held up his hand to give him a high five.

"So . . . a new manager." I cleared my throat, hoping to change the subject.

"Hopefully it goes well. We won't be long." Tucker leaned in and kissed my forehead. "Dorris picked her out, so it shouldn't be too hard a decision."

With that, the guys filed out of the bus, and I was left alone again. I wondered if it would always be this way—brief pockets with Tucker while he drifted in and out on official band business. I would definitely need to take up a hobby, otherwise I was going to go out of my mind. Plus, I refused to be just a trophy girlfriend—I knew I was worth more than that.

I flipped open the notebook again and sat back down at the table. For nearly twenty minutes I stared at the words I had written before deciding this cramped space wasn't conducive to creativity. I grabbed the book and pen and stepped out into the bright parking lot. I squinted as I scanned the rows of cars, looking for somewhere a little more private. I rounded the back of the bus and found another, smaller bus parked behind ours. I was sure it was Fifth's, but it was still, silent, and I figured they had gone out as well. I slid down against the back of our bus and placed my notebook on my lap as I began to jot down a few more lines. Memories of my past flooded my thoughts.

The smell of whiskey and cigarettes filled my nose, replacing the sweet smell of freedom. My hands flew to the back of my head as I struggled to pry Jackson's fingers from my hair. "Jax, let go of me!" I struggled to get my footing as he lifted me from the bed by my hair. His dirty fingers gripped onto my throat, cutting off my pleas for help. I stared into the lifeless bloodshot eyes of my boyfriend, silently pleading for him to let me go.

"Where is my dope?" he asked, his words slurring as his grip tightened. I clawed at his fingers, desperate for a gasp of air. "I know you fucking took it." I struggled to shake my head as my body grew weak. He released me, flinging my body back on the bed. I struggled to take in deep breaths as he loomed over me, waiting for an answer.

"I didn't. I wouldn't," I protested as I waited for his blows.

Lying crumpled and broken on empty sheets, feel the pain settle deep within me
I stand to fight another day, bracing for the blows on shaky legs
I take this pen and find my voice, fill the sheets with words of noise
My heart races to set the beat, as I bare my soul on empty sheets

"Plotting out world domination?" a female voice called from the window of the bus in front of me.

"I'm still in the early planning stages," I called back to Sarah who smiled and slid the window closed before appearing in the doorway of the bus.

"I needed to get out of there. It's like a coffin." She sighed as she gathered her dark hair and pulled it back into a hair tie. "Where are the guys?" she asked as she sank down next to me.

"At a meeting with a possible new manager," I replied as I chewed on the end of my pen.

"Yikes." She laughed as she picked up a pebble and tossed it toward her bus. "Well, you are just in time for the show."

I cocked my head to the side, not understanding what she meant until the door to the bus flew open again and Lizzy stepped outside. She had a cigarette dangling from her lips, and her hair was a wild mess of curls.

"Wow. . . ."

"I thought you would find that interesting. She shacked up with Derek last night. The sounds coming from his bunk would give you nightmares." She laughed. "At one point I wondered where they had gotten a goat."

I chuckled as I stared up at Lizzy whose eyes landed on me and anger flashed through them.

"What are you looking at?" she spat as she lit her cigarette. "You think you're better than me just because you're banging a lead singer?" She laughed as she shook her head. "I've already had him. You're not that special."

She reminded me of Cadence, Tucker's ex-girlfriend. She

was desperate to cling to anyone else's coattails instead of building a meaningful relationship, and she didn't care who she had to step on to get there. It made me sick to see the desperation in her eyes as she tried to pull me down with her.

Her words cut through me like a knife, and I could feel all happiness seeping out of the wound. I tried to form a response, but I couldn't speak. I was right back in the lobby of that hotel when I saw Tucker with his ex-girlfriend. My heart stopped in my chest as I saw Lizzy's eyes lock onto mine. I was an obstacle, not a person, and my feelings meant nothing. I had taken her words to heart, believed that I wasn't good enough for him and was only a placeholder until the next best thing came along. But those were my own insecurities, not how Tucker really saw me. Still, in the heat of the moment it was incredibly hard not to believe I wasn't good enough. It was something that had been drilled into me for years and not an easy notion to let go of.

"Don't believe me? I think my favorite picture in his bunk is the one of him on his bike."

Sarah pushed to her feet and was in front of Lizzy before I could absorb what she had just said to me.

"The free ride stops here. Get your shit, and get the hell off my bus," Sarah yelled as she folded her arms over her chest.

"Screw both of you!" Lizzy yelled back as she stormed onto the bus to gather her things. I pushed to my feet and made my way to the front of our bus. I needed to lie down, to think. I felt like my head was going to explode. I tossed my notebook on the floor and slipped into Tucker's bunk. My eyes danced over the pictures Tucker had taped to the top of the bed. My vision clouded over with tears as I looked up at a picture of him straddling his motorcycle.

"Cass?" Sarah called from the entrance of the bus. I didn't respond. I was afraid the floodgates would open and I would completely lose control of myself.

"You have to trust him to make this work. Tucker's a good guy."

"Tucker wouldn't . . ." I began, but my voice cracked.

"You're damn right he wouldn't. He loves you, and he loves Terry."

"The picture is right here."

"There is an explanation. You need to be stronger. You can't let her manipulate how you feel this easily."

"I am just so scared that I will wake up and everything with Tucker will all have been a dream."

It reminded me of all the times I had dreamed my father had come back and was now part of my life. I'd run through the scenario a thousand times in my mind wondering what it would be like, but it always ended in disappointment when I woke the next morning. I was scared that one day I would wake up and find that Tucker had never really come back to find me and I was just torturing myself.

"That's good. I'm going to write that down."

I pushed open the curtain and saw Sarah reaching for my notebook. I held my breath as her eyes scanned what I'd written.

"This is amazing, Cass. You have a way with words." She smiled up at me as she folded the notebook closed and handed it to me. I slid it under Tucker's pillow. "That would make a killer song."

"Thanks." I smiled, pride beginning to bolster my spirits again.

Sarah stood and began to make her way to the front of the bus.

"Sarah?"

She stopped, turning to look back at me.

"Thanks for talking some sense into me. . . . I . . . I don't know what I was thinking."

"You're only human. If it makes you feel better, I can chase down Lizzy and kick her ass." She winked, and I laughed.

"Maybe later." I watched her leave before flopping back on the pillow and staring up at the pictures of Tucker. He had been the one person in my life who didn't judge me and wanted nothing more than to see me smile. I needed to stop comparing everyone to my absent father and abusive ex-boyfriend. I knew better than to think of Jackson as my eyes grew heavy.

The living room was so trashed I could barely push the front door open after my long shift at the diner. My eyes scanned the mess and the two men who lay passed out on either end of the couch. I stepped over a plate and began to make my way back down the hall. When I heard a female giggle from the bathroom, I paused with my hand on the doorknob to my room. That wasn't my mother's voice, not that I had heard her laughter in years. It was someone much younger.

I walked to the bathroom door and listened as I heard Jax say something in a hushed tone. I shoved open the door and gasped as I saw a girl around my age sitting on his lap. The needle in his hand didn't register. All I saw was his arms looped around another woman.

"What are you doing?" My words broke under my shaky voice as I struggled not to break down and cry. I didn't want to be weak.

"Creating a new customer base." He smirked and shook the needle in his hand.

I felt ill, and my hand fell to my stomach as I struggled not to vomit the one meal I had been lucky enough to eat that day.

"You can't do this." I took a step inside the cramped bathroom, wishing I had found him cheating instead of ruining this poor girl's life. "Come on." I held out my hand to the brunette who sat perched on my boyfriend's knee. She drew into him and glared at my hand.

"I'm not going anywhere. He wants me here, so you can

just fuck off," she spat angrily. Jax laughed, finding the
whole exchange amusing.

"Cass!" My eyes fluttered open to the sound of Tucker's voice. I sat up, wrapping my arms around his neck and pulling him against me. "Shh . . ." He stroked my hair as I held on to him. "It was just a bad dream, sweetheart. I'm here."

"It felt so real."

"He can't hurt you anymore."

I nodded into his shoulder as I lifted my gaze to see the rest of the band standing silently around us.

"I'm so sorry." I pulled back from Tucker and wiped the tears from my cheeks, embarrassed.

"You have nothing to be sorry about, Cass." Tucker glanced over his shoulder to the other guys. They all nodded in agreement.

CHAPTER

Seven

I LOCKED MYSELF IN the cramped bathroom of the bus, waiting for the humiliation of my nightmare to pass. I couldn't look at my own reflection in the mirror because that scared little girl from the trailer park might be staring back at me.

There was a soft knock at the door, and I hesitated before sliding open the small pocket door.

"We were thinking of going out for a bite to eat," Eric said as he leaned against the wall.

"Sure. I'll see you guys later." I forced the lump in my throat down as I began to pull the door closed. He stuck his hand out, stopping me as he laughed.

"We aren't going without you. You're part of this family, too." He shook his head as he took a step back. "Get ready, woman. Powder your shit or whatever it is you chicks do. I'm starving." His hand rubbed over his stomach before he walked toward the front of the bus.

I smiled as I glanced back at the small mirror over the sink, this time boldly taking in my reflection. I needed to stop living in the past. I had moved on from that broken, shattered shell of the girl who lived in the trailer park—I had embarked on a new chapter and, for the first time, I allowed myself to pause for a moment and take it all in. My thoughts briefly drifted to Sarah. Watching her onstage last night, I was instantly intimidated by the way she took control and demanded attention from the crowd. That was something I needed to learn to do in my own life. Sarah was right—I needed to figure out what I wanted to do and who I wanted to be. My dreams had changed so much in the last year that I wasn't sure what I wanted out of my life. I knew I wanted Tucker by my side; that was a given. But I also wanted to have my own identity. Leaving the trailer park was not the end of my dreams.

"Where are we going?" I asked as I stepped into the tiny hallway of the bus.

"Chinese," Terry called from the front of the bus.

"Pizza," Chris said, shoving his brother in the shoulder.

"We could hit the food court in the mall. They have a little bit of everything," I called out, and all eyes turned to me. Tucker hooked his arm around my neck and kissed me on the temple.

"I love you." His breath tickled my ear and sent a shiver all the way down to my toes.

"I love you, too."

"All right. Let's not make us all sick before we even eat," Eric yelled, but he was smiling; a rare sight.

We made our way to the mall, laughing together in one cohesive group, and I was filled again with a new sense of hope. Maybe they were starting to let me in.

I ordered a milk shake and burger from Mooers and Shakers as the guys spread out to order their food.

"You want me to take that?" Tucker asked as he grabbed a fry from my tray and popped it into his mouth.

"I think I can handle it, Tucker," I replied as he made a face when the fry burnt his tongue. We picked a corner booth away from the chaos of the teenage girls who crowded the mall.

"I know you can. I like doing things for you."

"You've done enough."

"A lover's quarrel? Dinner and a show." Eric sat his tray at the end of the booth and grabbed a chair from a neighboring table, turning it backward to straddle it.

"We aren't fighting." I blew on a fry before biting off the end.

"Shame. Tuck writes better when he is all sad and bitchy. The lovey-dovey shit is hell on his creativity." He laughed and Tucker smacked him on the chest.

"I think we've had enough sad times to last us a lifetime." My eyes fell on the twins as they slid into the bench seat across from us.

"My writing doesn't hold a candle to Cass's." Tucker grabbed his slice of pizza from his plate and took a bite.

I laughed nervously as I took a bite from my burger.

"I'll be the judge of that. Lay it on us." Eric folded his hands together, giving me his undivided attention.

"You're out of your damn mind! How did the meeting go?" I asked the twins, wanting to divert the attention from me.

"It was all right. If you have some new material for us, we wouldn't mind taking a look," Terry replied. So much for diverting attention.

"I don't know how to write songs. It's more of a poem."

"Same difference," Chris said, and the others nodded in agreement.

"So do you have a new manager or what?"

Tucker shrugged and dropped his pizza on his plate, grabbing a napkin to wipe his mouth. Eric watched him for a minute before responding.

"I think she would be good for us," he responded, and Tucker sat back in his seat, lacing his hands behind his head.

"You don't agree?" I put my hand on Tucker's thigh and felt him tense beneath my fingers.

"She's younger and more into our scene." He shrugged.

"So what's the problem?' I asked as I looked around at the others.

"She wants to fast-track our careers. She has lots of ideas," Chris replied.

"That doesn't sound so bad." My eyes moved to Terry.

"She's made huge deals in the past for other bands, like Lip and Crawl Space."

"That's great. I'm not seeing the problem."

Eric grinned as he tossed his crumpled napkin on his half-eaten food.

"She doesn't think it's wise to have groupies . . . or girl-friends . . . on the road with us." His smirk faded, and I knew he wasn't being an asshole.

"Oh." I sat back in my seat and glanced over at Tucker.

"It's not going to fucking happen. Either Cass stays with me, or I don't go." The muscles in Tucker's jaw ticked.

"Nobody wants Cass to leave," Terry replied, and I felt marginally better, but the pit in my stomach felt like it was going to consume me.

"So we hire her. She can be an assistant or personal shopper or some shit." Eric was actually throwing out ideas to keep me around? I couldn't help but smile.

"A writer," Chris suggested.

"I'm not a writer." I shook my head as I chewed on the end of my milk shake straw.

"You really think it's wise to hire a manager who is already gonna start out with drama?" Tucker grabbed my hand from his leg and squeezed it.

"She's good at what she does. This was what we've been needing; this is what's going to be the difference between local gigs and sold-out arenas," Eric almost shouted. The tension was beginning to build again, and I felt like I needed to help defuse the situation.

Tucker cut his eyes to Chris, and I rubbed my thumb over the back of his hand to try to calm him.

"Nothing against Dorris, man. She was great, but she doesn't know a lot about this scene," Chris explained.

Everyone was silent for a moment.

"I'll show you my poem, if you think it'll help convince her that I'm worth keeping around. And if you guys like it, it's yours." I kept my eyes on my burger as I waited for a response.

"You sure, sweetheart?" Tucker asked as he adjusted in his seat.

"Yeah, I want to help you guys." I shrugged and sat my milk shake down on the table. "I think I'm stuffed."

We made our way back to the bus, and the guys took turns getting themselves ready for their concert while I sat in Tucker's bunk and let the memories of my past flood me. I wanted this song to feel real, unvarnished, the way Tucker's songs did. I wanted this to be more than just some words on a piece of paper.

I pictured my mother and her struggle to follow her dreams in life as my father criticized her and told her she wasn't good enough. I wondered what he would think of my life now and if he would be proud that I was no longer living in the situation I had been or if he would try to discourage me from following my dreams as well.

The truth is told through blurred vision, this is the world that I must live in

I wondered if he had changed at all from the man I remembered him as and if he regretted his decision to leave his family behind only to have Jax step in and fill his shoes. I blamed myself every day for the way things had ended. If I had only been honest, maybe things would not have had such a violent end, or maybe it would have only come sooner.

I've lost everything to you, but these words will get me through

Tears filled my eyes as I thought of what life would be like now if I hadn't lost the baby. Would I be a good mother? Would history have continued to repeat itself? I would never know unless I was able to get back to where it all began, but my father was long gone, abandoning hope for our family and dooming it in the process. I would never get the answers to the questions that weighed me down.

If you take this life from me, I will fly with broken wings
Let me fill these empty sheets, with those lies of love you told
to me

Tears began to fall on the paper, blurring the ink as I gave in to the sadness. It was therapeutic to tell my side of the story. Sarah was right; everyone should have a creative outlet to express their emotions. It amazed me how easily it came to me as I scribbled line after line. Once I started writing, I couldn't stop. Maybe this was my purpose—to write. To share my pain, not only to heal myself, but maybe to help heal others.

"You okay?" Tucker asked as he held back the curtain to the bed.

"I'm fine. This is good." I nodded and sniffled, giving him a small smile. He smiled back, his eyes filling with sadness before he let the curtain fall back into place.

My mother always seemed to hold out hope that things would get better, and I wished she would have lived long enough to see that they had. I no longer feared what tomorrow would bring, but the loss of her weighed heavy in my heart, and I felt guilty that I was able to move on with my life, leaving everyone else behind.

Angels have found their wings from you,
battered and bruised when they come through

Maybe I didn't have a choice in the way it all ended. Maybe the course my life was on had been predetermined and the only control I had was how I handled the situations as they came my way.

> *This world was cruel and unforgiving,*
> *not fit for angels to live in*
> *Said I would never be alone,*
> *lying on empty sheets in a place that's not my home*

I closed the notebook, and my eyes drifted up to the pictures of Tucker plastered to the roof of the bunk, reminding me that I was safe now, that that life was behind me, reminding me of the man who helped pull me out of that life and into this new one.

I slid out of the bunk, chewing on my lip as I walked to the table at the front of the bus. I dropped the notebook in front of Tucker, and his eyes drifted up to meet mine.

"I'm gonna step outside and get some air." I turned and left the bus, suddenly feeling vulnerable and terrified. I couldn't bear to hear what they had to say about my writing—I felt like I'd left a piece of my soul behind on that table, poised for their evisceration. Lyrics are their livelihood, and if they don't like them, they won't hesitate to tell me.

The sun was beginning to set, but the air was still muggy and holding on to the heat of the day. I was so nervous I contemplated going to a store and getting a pack of cigarettes, but I knew I would never hear the end of it from Tucker, so I continued to chew on my lip as I waited for what felt like a lifetime.

Finally the door swung open, and Tucker stepped down off the steps of the bus. I didn't look at him as I fidgeted with the hem of my T-shirt.

I searched his face for some sort of reaction as he came to my side and leaned against the bus.

"It's really fucking hard to read about what happened to you." He kicked a few stones with his shoe. "But you did an amazing job."

"What do the guys think?"

"They love it. Terry and Chris are already trying to figure out the beat to the song."

"Really?" I finally allowed myself to look up at him. He was smiling, clearly finding my insecurity amusing.

"I meant what I said earlier. If this manager wants you gone, I'm leaving with you."

"I won't let you do that."

"You don't have a choice. I can't live without you, Cass. Not again."

I nodded and wrapped my arms around his neck. I loved how he fought for us, even when I didn't think it was the best thing for him to do. His hand ran up and down my spine before he pulled back to look me in the eye.

"I love you more than anything. I know it's hard for you to believe that, sweetheart, but I am willing to do anything to prove it to you."

"I know you love me, Tucker. So much."

The rest of the band began to file out of the bus, and I reluctantly pulled back from our embrace.

"Good job, Cass." Chris placed his hand on my shoulder as
he walked by. I beamed. Maybe I really had found my calling.

CHAPTER

Eight

HE CONCERT WAS in full effect, and the air was buzzing with excitement backstage. The show would be twice the size of last night's. Filth was just finishing up their set.

"Break a leg out there." I gave Tucker a kiss on the cheek as Eric made gagging sounds from behind us. I rolled my eyes and shot him the finger behind Tucker's back.

"I'll see you soon." We could hear the crowd roar from backstage. "That's our cue."

Sarah approached me with a wicked grin.

"What are you up to?" Tucker gave me a look of concern. I shook my head, no clue what she was planning.

"Girl time." Sarah looped her arm in mine and pulled me from Tucker's side. I shot him an apologetic look as she dragged me off to the hallway.

"Love you," I mouthed, and Tucker winked at me as they disappeared in the opposite direction.

I focused my attention on the sweaty and overly excited rock star who was dragging me off into the unknown.

"Where are we going?" I asked as she shot me a smile.

"I figured after the drama, you could use a little pampering."

I pulled back from her, but she kept a firm grip on my arm.

"Every girl needs to be pampered, and I don't ever get to do this stuff." She gave me her best puppy-dog eyes.

We slipped inside a closed door marked PRIVATE.

"What is this place?"

"Hair and makeup." She was beaming with excitement. "Sit."

"This is going to be a disaster." I sat down in a chair in front of a large oval mirror.

"That's the spirit!" Sarah stood behind me, sinking down so her face was next to mine as she inspected my reflection. "I can work with this."

I giggled as I rolled my eyes, propping my feet up on the bar below the mirrored stand.

"So how is the writing going?" she asked as she grabbed a brush and began running it over my hair.

"Hold still, Cassie. Mommy can't braid your hair if you keep squirming like a worm in your seat!" The memories of my mother flooded my thoughts, and I was overwhelmed with how much I missed

the little moments we had together. I wished I had told her how much those times meant to me before she died.

"Hello? Earth to Cass!"

"Sorry. I wrote a song . . . I think. The guys really liked it. They want to play it."

Sarah made a face letting me know she was impressed.

"Well aren't you big-time now?" She gathered my hair and pulled it back with a hair tie. "How do you feel about makeup?"

"Repulsed."

"Good enough. I am going to paint you up like a movie star." Sarah spun my chair around to face her. "No peeking until I'm done."

"You're wasting your time. It's like putting lipstick on a pig." I laughed and actually snorted.

"You don't have many female friends, do you?" She raised an eyebrow as she grabbed some sort of base coat to slather on my face.

"Do you?"

"None," she said as she began to rub the creamy concoction over my cheeks. "It's nice to have you here."

I smiled, feeling exactly the same way.

"Now stop grinning or you're gonna look like the Joker."

I let her paint my face as we talked about love and relationships. I told her the story of how Tucker and I met, leaving out the most gruesome details of our relationship. She told me about her relationship with Derek and how it took them months to be able to be around each other after it ended. In the end, she felt the breakup was the best thing for them and the band.

"What do you think of Eric?" I asked as she pulled my hair down and ran her fingers through it, deciding which style she wanted to try.

"He's . . . cute." Her cheeks blushed.

"I think he likes you. When he looks at you, it is the only time he doesn't look like he is plotting out someone's murder." I closed my eyes as her fingers rubbed over my scalp, separating my hair into sections.

"Too bad our band has a policy not to get involved with other bands." She shrugged like it was no big deal, but I could tell it upset her.

"Who better than someone who has a passion for the same things you do?" I asked.

"The guys would kill me. How do you feel about curls?"

"They're okay, I guess. You're changing the subject."

"How would you feel if you broke up with Tucker and still had to work with him? Would you be able to see him with someone else?"

"I think it would break my heart all over again."

"Exactly. I keep my mouth shut about Derek and his groupies, but it still hurts. I understand why he doesn't want to see me with one of these other guys. I get it." Sarah began to curl small sections of my hair as we chatted. I could completely understand her situation, but I couldn't imagine how lonely it must be for her.

"Can I look in the mirror?" I asked, craning my neck as it began to stiffen.

"No! It would spoil all the fun! I want it to be a surprise!"

"I hate surprises."

"Not all surprises are bad." She laughed as she pulled another section free to curl.

"Fine, I'll wait," I smirked. "But I am not happy about it."

"Duly noted." Sarah continued to work her fingers through my hair, bringing my thoughts back to my mother. It was one of the few fond memories I had of her. It was also one of the worst when I looked back at the way my father had put her down and prevented her from following her dreams.

"You look like a princess," my mother praised me as she finished curling my hair. I ran off to my room to pull on my favorite dress, excited to surprise my father for his birthday. He had been at work all day and was due home two hours ago. After checking the clock for the hundredth time, she finally took my hand and walked me down to O'Brian's, a local bar that Daddy sometimes went to after work to unwind with his friends.

As we walked through the door, she stopped, trying to pull me back outside, but I saw my dad sitting at the bar. I pulled my hand free from hers and ran to him. He was shocked but surprised when I yelled happy birthday.

"This certainly is a surprise." His eyes narrowed as they locked on

Momma who was still standing by the door, tears falling down her cheeks.

"I'll call you later," he said quickly to the woman sitting next to him. I hadn't even noticed she was there, but Momma did, and she didn't look very happy.

"I think we are just about done." Sarah squealed and clasped her hands together.

"Can I see?"

She made a face as she thought it over before shaking her head no.

"I think you need a new outfit."

"I don't really have anything . . ." I let my voice trail off as Sarah's eyes began to sparkle.

"You can borrow something of mine. I have the perfect outfit."

"I don't think I could fit in your clothes." I sunk back against the chair.

"Whatever! You're like ten pounds thinner than me. My clothes will look hot on you. Come on. Tucker will be offstage soon!"

I reluctantly pushed from my seat and followed Sarah through the maze of halls and to her tour bus. I folded my arms over my chest and tapped my foot like a stubborn child as she dug through her cabinet full of clothing, tossing shirts and skirts behind her as she sifted through the mess.

"Perfect!" She held up a dress and spun around to face me.

Between her fingers was a scrap of fabric that I couldn't be certain was a doily or an old fancy handkerchief like the one Larry used to blow his nose in at the diner.

"Where is the rest of it?"

Sarah frowned as she looked from the dress to me.

"You don't like it?"

"I mean, I'm sure you look hot in it. It's just . . . not me." I began to fidget, picking at my fingernail nervously. Sarah's shoulders slumped, and she sighed dramatically.

"Tell me who you are Cass." Her eyebrow raised as she challenged me.

"I don't know. I'm a waitress." I began to mentally tick off the things in my head that I thought defined who I was.

"You're not a waitress . . . or at least not a good one. You have been missing an awful lot of work." She laughed, and I narrowed my eyes at her.

"Okay . . . I'm just plain."

"Plain?" she asked like the word left a bad taste in her mouth.

"Yeah." I stuck out my chin defiantly.

"You happy with being *plain*?"

I shrugged my shoulders, not sure how I could respond honestly and not lose the argument.

"Ughh . . . fine. I'll try on the stupid napkin." I grabbed the dress from her hand, and she stuck her tongue out at me in victory. I rolled my eyes, and she pointed to the door that hid the master bedroom at the back of the bus. I slid it open and my hands flew up to cover my mouth at the sight of naked, writhing bodies that suddenly appeared before my eyes. Sarah stood frozen by my side like a deer in headlights before she grabbed my arm, digging her nails in just a little too deep as she yanked me back down the hallway and off the bus. As soon as we hit the warm nighttime air, she hunched over, hands on her knees as she struggled to control her breathing.

"What . . ." That was the only word I could choke out. Sarah just shook her head as her breathing now sounded more like sobs. I placed my hand on her back, hesitantly, trying to soothe her. It was then that I put two and two together that her ex-boyfriend had been in that tangle of bodies in the back of the bus. "I'm sorry." I wasn't used to anyone needing my help or wanting my comfort. It was an odd feeling. I gripped Sarah's forearms and pulled her back up to a standing position as she swiped away the tears that had mixed with charcoal-black eyeliner and run down her face.

"Come on. You can come on our bus." She nodded, and I kept my arms around her as I guided her to the other side of the monstrous vehicle and pulled open the door for her.

As soon as we were inside and alone I sat her at the small kitchen table.

"Do you want to talk about it?" I asked, sliding into the seat across from her. She shook her head as every negative emotion flashed through her eyes. She scratched over a faded tattoo on the underside of her arm, leaving white lines of damaged skin across its surface. She looked desperate and heartbroken.

"You're not really over him, are you?" I asked, hoping to open a line of communication.

"Is it that obvious?" She laughed sadly as she stared down at her tattoo.

"Was that for him?"

"It was . . . but I honestly think it was more for me. If I put him on me permanently, maybe he couldn't leave, ya know? That sounds stupid."

"It's not stupid. Can I see?" I held out my hand to take her arm. She hesitated before extending her arm to me so I could look over the design. "Rock?" I asked as I read over the script.

"He was my rock. He kept me grounded." She rolled her eyes and smiled, "And rock and roll was something we had in common." I could see her mood lighten as the memories washed over her and her fingers traced the script.

"I like it. Very clever." I stared down at her arm. As the pink lines from her nails began to fade, I could clearly see old scars beneath it. "What is that?" I tried to keep any judgment from my expression.

"Nothing." She pulled her arm back and slipped it below the table. "Are you gonna try that on or what? The guys will be back any minute."

"Yeah." I lifted the little black dress before pushing up from the table and making my way down the hall to Dorris's old room. "The bathroom is right there if you want to fix your mascara." I pointed to the tiny bathroom beside me before I disappeared into the bedroom.

I slipped off my clothes as I wondered how Sarah had gotten those marks on her arm. I held the dress up in front of me as I tried to figure out how the hell to put it on. I wiggled my arms between two thin straps and slipped it over my head. I'd never worn anything so tight . . . or that left so little to the imagination. It dipped low in the chest, rose high on the thigh, and the back was nonexistent.

I wiggled my feet back into my sandals and let out a long, frustrated sigh. I wasn't sure who I was, but *this* wasn't it. It was so far out of my comfort zone I needed a passport to wear it.

"Stop second-guessing yourself, and get your sexy little ass out here," Sarah yelled, louder than necessary.

"I don't think this is me." I frowned as I tugged on the hem of the sorry excuse for a dress.

"You who? The waitress? Come on. Live a little. You may discover there is more to you than that girl you left behind." Sarah tugged me into the cramped bathroom, her body pressed between the wall and my back as she smiled into the mirror in front of me. As my eyes left hers and drifted over myself, my breath caught in my throat. I didn't recognize the girl staring back at me. Scratch that, it was a *woman* staring back at me, and she was hot.

"How in the hell did you do that?" I leaned over the sink, inspecting my flawless makeup. I was certain Sarah was going to paint me up like I belonged in one of the bands, but instead it looked . . . natural. I still felt like me.

"Tucker is going to go crazy." Her lips pulled up in a smile, but her eyes were full of sadness.

"I don't think Eric is going to mind finding you in his bus either." I laughed as she pinched my side, causing me to squirm.

"Come on. I'm sure he is elbow-deep in groupies."

"No." I shook my head as I thought back to the little time I had spent with Eric. "I honestly think he enjoys being all miserable and cranky."

"Well, he is in good company then."

"You know, if you ever want to talk about it . . ."

Sarah brushed a curl from my face and grabbed my arm, pulling me from the tiny room.

"Let's go see if we can catch the guys as they come offstage."

She dragged me out of the bus and into the packed building that was now overflowing with groupies and fans. I felt like I was naked in a room full of people. I let my hair fall over my face to help hide myself as we twisted through the maze of halls and through security.

Damaged was finishing up the last song of their set, and as I listened to Tucker's smooth voice sing about love, I completely forgot what I was so worried about. Sarah and I sang along. We swayed to the music as Sarah stared at Eric with a far-off look in her eye.

"I see you staring," I joked as I bumped her with my shoulder. She shot me a playful glare, tucking her hair behind her ear.

"Nothing in the rules about looking."

The chorus faded out as the crowd grew impossibly loud, begging for an encore. Tucker waved to the crowd and thanked them for coming, and as his eyes fell on me, his words caught in his throat. I could feel the blush crawl over my body from my toes all the way to my cheeks as his lips curled up in a flirtatious grin.

"Maybe one more song. How does that sound?" He spoke into the microphone and everyone went wild. Sarah and I yelled and clapped along with them, getting lost in the moment. Tucker turned to the band and they all nodded before they began to play. It took a moment to recognize the song as it was being played with guitars and a steady tapping of the drum, but when Tucker began to sing, my heart melted.

Visions of the first time Tucker and I had made love flashed in my thoughts, and I could tell by the look in his eye that he was lost in the memory of us together as well.

I had a big dopey grin plastered across my face as he sang the last line in front of thousands of people, but I was the only one he saw. I had never felt so treasured and beautiful as I did when I saw the way Tucker looked at me.

We were a million miles from our turbulent past, and I couldn't wait to be even further into our future. The idea of a family of our own still terrified me, but I had no doubt in my mind that when that time did come, Tucker would be an amazing father. All of my worries and fears of coming on this tour washed away.

As he stepped down from the stage, he hesitated, his eyes taking in the tiny black dress. His fingers slid over my hip, and he squeezed gently.

"You look incredible." His tongue rolled over his lips and warmth spread from my belly as his eyes darkened.

"You signing, Tuck?" Terry called from behind us, and Tucker let his forehead fall against mine as he closed his eyes and took a deep breath.

"Don't you go anywhere," he said as he took a step back and made his way to his fans.

CHAPTER

Nine

"GOOD GUYS FINISH last." Terry laughed, hitting Eric on the chest. "Ain't that right, Cass?"

"Um . . . I don't know." I shrugged.

"Don't be such a fucking pervert," Sarah scolded him before her gaze landed on Eric. "They do if they want to hit it again." She winked, and he grinned wickedly back at her as Tucker slid between them. His hand gripped the side of my neck, and he pulled my lips against his in a sensual kiss. My knees went weak and his other hand looped around my lower back and he held me against him as his tongue slid across my lower lip.

"How am I supposed to keep my hands off you when you wear things like this?" He cocked his head to the side as his eyes danced over my barely concealed body.

"It was Sarah's idea." I tucked a curl behind my ear.

"Smart girl."

Sarah patted Tucker on the back as she and the guys walked by us to head backstage. His hand slid lower onto my butt, and he gave it a gentle squeeze.

"You're going to miss your party." I looped my arms around his neck, desperate to be closer.

"Fuck the party."

I pushed my lips against his, letting my fingers tangle in his dark messy hair. He groaned against my mouth, and I could feel how badly he wanted me as he pushed his hips against mine.

"If she won't fuck you, I will, Tucker," a crazy fan screamed from the other side of the guardrail, effectively ruining our romantic moment.

"I'm sorry," he whispered in my ear with his cheek pressed against mine. I closed my eyes, inhaling coconut and soap before taking a step back. I hated not being able to hug and kiss my boyfriend in public. It was definitely something that would take some getting used to.

Tucker gave me an apologetic look as he took my hand, lacing our fingers together and pulling me toward the door to backstage.

The party was in full swing, and bodies spilled into every hall. Tucker placed his arm over my shoulder and kept me tucked into his side as we navigated our way to the main room. It didn't take long to locate the band. Chris was standing on a chair and yelling out dirty jokes to anyone who would listen, which, unsurprisingly, was a lot of girls in skimpy clothes. I suspected that he could recite the dictionary and they would still be in awe.

My self-consciousness flew out the window as I watched a woman bouncing topless on the shoulders of Derek from Filth. My heart sank, and I hoped that Sarah was not anywhere near him.

"What's wrong?"

I realized I was squeezing Tucker's hand and relaxed my grip.

"Just worried about Sarah."

Tucker nodded, running his hand over his hair from back to front.

"What is it?" I asked, angling toward him so I could read his face.

"Nothing."

"What?"

Tucker sighed and took a step back from me, his eyes going to the drop ceiling before landing back on me.

"She's an awesome chick, and I am glad you have found a friend."

"But?" I took a step closer to him.

"She's had it rough, and she can get kind of . . . intense."

I laughed and I saw his face change from concerned to downright confused.

"She's had it rough?" I asked, making sure I had heard him correctly.

"Look, I know you didn't have it easy either, and you

turned out just fine. More than fine. But not everyone handles stress and heartache the way you do. I'm not saying she is a bad person. She's a cool chick."

I cocked an eyebrow at his choice of words and he rolled his eyes.

"You know what I mean. She's a nice person. Just be careful. She tends to push people away."

"I'll be careful." I leaned forward and placed a kiss on his cheek. "Thanks for looking out for me."

"That's my job." Tucker looped his arm around my neck and pulled my head to his as we continued to navigate through the crowd.

"I don't need anyone to take care of me," I reminded him as my eyes fell on Sarah and Eric.

"Yeah, I know. You have told me that before," he joked as he followed my gaze, and the smile slipped from his face.

"You have a problem with those two getting together?"

His arm flexed behind my neck and I knew the answer to my question.

"Those two are a ticking fucking time bomb, sweetheart. Don't say I didn't warn you." As soon as the words left his mouth, he nodded to Eric who returned the gesture. "Let's go watch the train wreck."

On our path to the others we grabbed a few beers from some random groupie who had no problem running her hand over the front of my boyfriend's jeans while his arms were around me. He took a step back out of her reach. I raised my glass and Tucker placed his arm in front of mine, keeping me from spilling my beer all over her, but the look on his face was one of amusement.

"She has it coming." I tipped the cup to my lips and downed half the contents in a single gulp.

"Choose your battles wisely. We have had enough to last us a lifetime." He tilted his cup to his lips and took a drink.

"I know. I'm sorry. This is a lot to get used to."

"Trust me. I get it." We had made our way to Sarah and E and we both said hello politely. "Just remember who is bunking with me tonight."

"Oh, shit. I don't want to listen to that shit." Eric looked revolted.

"You can stay on our bus," Sarah suggested as she took a drink from her cup.

"Yeah, I'm sure Derek would give you a warm welcome," Tucker said to no one in particular. He was right. Sarah and Derek had a volatile relationship, and the last thing Damaged needed was a rift between them and their opening act. We still had to finish out this tour in some measure of peace.

"Fuck Derek," Eric replied, and Tucker clenched his jaw. Eric was the type of guy that went against the grain and refused to listen to reason.

"'Fuck Derek'?" a voice called from behind us, and I was thankful that it was Terry and not another member of Filth.

I could tell it rattled Sarah who slid farther away from Eric.

"You need a refill?" I asked over the music that began to fill the awkward silence.

"Sure." She smiled as she grabbed my hand, tugging me out of Tucker's arms. I didn't want to have any part of Damaged's heated conversations, and I knew Sarah had realized that she had placed Eric in a bad position.

"What are you doing?" I asked when we had gotten far enough away that we weren't in danger of being overheard.

"I just want what you and Tuck have. It's not fair." She was clearly already drunk, but she still grabbed a bottle of Jack and poured a few shots into her glass, holding the bottle up to offer me some. I shrugged and let her fill my solo cup about halfway with the amber liquid.

"I get it." I took a small drink, cringing at the nasty warmth of the alcohol.

"My ex is dictating my happiness. It's not fair. I just want to be able to live my life and be happy."

"I've been there. Trust me. I had a pretty rocky relationship before Tucker." I relaxed my throat and took a bigger drink, wishing I hadn't brought up my past.

"Yeah? How'd you get him to leave you alone?"

"Tucker killed him." All of the air left my lungs, and I immediately regretted my words.

"You are so twisted." She laughed and downed her shots in one sip.

I was thankful she assumed I was joking and I wouldn't have to go into the horrid details of that final night with Jax.

"Another?" She grabbed the bottle, shaking it in her hand as the contents sloshed against the glass.

I glanced back at the guys who looked like they were still in the middle of a heated conversation, and I had no desire to play referee to a bunch of angry rockers.

"Absolutely," I yelled over the music as I held out my cup. A hand slinked up the back of my dress and caused me to jump, and the brown liquid poured over my hands. "What the hell?"

"Jesus, Cass, I'm sorry!" Sarah apologized for the mess, oblivious to why I was upset. I spun around and was face-to-chest with a man covered in tattoos and with a bull ring dangling from his nose.

"What the hell is wrong with you, asshole?" I yelled, gathering the attention of a few bystanders.

"Since when do groupies get upset when someone wants some ass? You don't have to be a fucking bitch." He laughed, sticking out his pierced tongue between his teeth.

"I'm not a groupie, you fucking pervert!" I pulled back my fist, fully intending to hit him right on that stupid target dangling from his face when Sarah shoved me aside and cracked him across his cheek. The sound of her slap was so loud that even the tattooed freak looked to me in stunned silence as he tried to figure out what the hell had just happened.

"Who's the bitch now?" Sarah was laughing like a maniac as she continued to taunt the guy. Tucker and the rest of the band had shoved anyone who was in their way aside and now were standing behind the ass-grabber looking positively livid. Great.

"It's fine. It's over," I yelled, holding out my hands to keep them back, but the guy had a death wish and turned around to face them, wiping his lip that had split against his teeth.

"Did he touch you?" Tucker looked around the man to me, not the least bit fazed by the way the guy was staring him down.

"Tucker . . ."

"Answer the question." He wasn't in the mood, and I certainly didn't want to be on the receiving end of his bad attitude, but I also wasn't going to let him get thrown in jail over this douche bag.

"It was a misunderstanding, and it's over." I looked to Sarah who nodded in agreement.

"See, just a misunderstanding," the guy chuckled. "Turns out she fucking liked it."

As the words left his mouth so did a spray of blood, followed by what looked like a tooth, but I couldn't be sure it wasn't the barbell from his tongue. Terry was on top of him the second he hit him, grabbing his shirt and yanking him toward the back door. A security guard pushed his way through the crowd of onlookers and grabbed the guy by the arm, yanking him away from Terry. Another joined him and together they hauled the jerk out of the back entrance. I didn't know what they did with him from there, but I was sure I wouldn't lose any sleep over it.

"Is this going to happen after every concert?"

Sarah laughed and shook her head, and we both looked at the band.

"I guess that means the party is over." Tucker ran his hand over his hair the way he always does when something is on his mind.

"We can hang out a little longer if you want." I shrugged, and Tucker gave me one of his heart-stopping smiles.

"Yeah? You haven't had enough of this yet?"

"That's what she said!" I yelled with a laugh and Sarah snorted.

"No, Cass. Just no." Eric put up his hand with a dead-serious look as he shook his head in mock disappointment.

"Whatever. That was a good one." The other guys laughed at me as they refilled their cups. I held mine out for a few more shots, my body already warming as the liquor spread throughout my veins.

Tucker wrapped his arms around my waist and rested his chin on my shoulder.

"I love this dress on you, but maybe it isn't such a good idea to have you walking around like that at the after-parties."

"I can take care of myself, Tucker." I rolled my eyes, knowing I was sounding like a broken record. He was only concerned for my safety, but he didn't need to be. I needed to learn how to be independent, fierce, like Sarah. He wouldn't always be able to stand up for me.

"I know you can take care of yourself." He turned me around in his arms. "But I don't want you to ever get hurt again. That motherfucker got off easy. I should have beaten his ass." His fingers slid along my jaw and over my lips. His gaze dipped to my mouth. I could feel the anger rolling off him in waves, but he tried to conceal it.

"Fine." I leaned in close to whisper in his ear. "You can take it off of me later." I pulled back just enough to see his expression. His eyes darkened and his eyes hooded and the muscle in his jaw ticked under the surface.

"You sure you're not ready to go back to the bus?" His mouth hovered over mine so I was breathing his air.

"Soon. I promise." I gave him a quick peck on the lips and took a step back.

Tucker emptied his cup and poured more alcohol inside. A song that I recognized came on the radio and my liquid courage had kicked in. I began to sway my hips and nod my head to the beat as Sarah grabbed my arm, nearly throwing me off balance.

"Let's dance!" she yelled a little too loudly in my ear. I winced in pain.

"I'm not much of a dancer."

"Come on. I want to show Eric what he is missing," she

whispered as she looked around me to Eric who was chatting up a groupie. "And who cares what anyone here thinks? Enjoy life. No one gets out alive."

"Fine. But don't have high expectations. I don't think I could walk straight, let alone keep rhythm."

"Are you kidding me? Look how some of these nutbags are wiggling around out there. I'm not sure if they are dancing or if we should call an ambulance." I let her tug me along as she made fun of the crazy outfits and questionable piercing choices of the other partiers. I was laughing so hard I was nearly in tears as she stopped, causing me to run into her back.

"Maybe you are a little too drunk for this." She turned around, looking at me like I had sprouted a horn.

"That's it. I'm going to have to break it down." I narrowed my eyes as I rotated my hips. Sarah laughed so hard no sound came out of her mouth.

"See how much fun you can have when you let your hair down? This is what it's all about. Screw what anyone else thinks or does. Make yourself happy. Live in the moment."

I stopped moving, absorbing all of the things she was telling me as alcohol fogged my brain.

"Ughh . . . dance!" Her fingers wrapped around my hips and she pulled me closer, guiding my body with her hands. I threw my hands above my head and yelled as I tossed my head to the side, curls falling over my face. I'd never let loose like this before, and I couldn't believe how good it felt to feel so free.

"This is so much fun!"

"See! I told you." She grabbed my hand and twirled me around playfully. My eyes caught Tucker's, and he still looked like he was dwelling on the asshole who had grabbed my ass. He also looked like he had drunk a few shots too many.

Sarah pressed her lips together in a thin line and cocked her head to the side when she saw my look of concern.

"He's fine. The guys party like this all of the time. Stop worrying so damn much."

I turned my back to her, pressing my bottom into her as we shimmied together. Tucker leaned back against the drink table, taking small sips of his drink, his eyes locked onto mine. Derek made his way through the crowd, bobbing his head to the music.

"You always knew how to move, Sarah." He shook his hair from his face. Sarah's body slowed behind me, and I heard her suck in a deep breath. "Can I cut in?"

I glanced over his shoulder to Tucker who slammed his cup down on the table and stood. The last time I had seen that look on his face, he was face-to-face with Jax.

"I'm gonna grab a drink." I glanced over my shoulder, looking for confirmation from Sarah that she was okay. She nodded slightly, and I slipped by Derek and made my way to Tucker.

"What was that about?" he asked before I could reach him.

"He wanted to dance with Sarah," I replied, irritated at what seemed like jealousy. Her name got the attention of Eric who spun to look at me before his eyes searched the dance floor. My stomach churned as he located her with her ex.

"I'm sorry, E." I let my shoulders sag as I gave him an apologetic glance.

"Why are you sorry?" He shrugged and drank the contents of his cup before crushing it in his fist. "She ain't shit to me." He flung the cup on the ground and slipped through the crowd of bodies.

"That really sucks." I turned my attention back to Tucker who didn't seem to register any of the conversation with Eric. "What is up with you?"

He took a deep breath as his eyes went unfocused.

"I feel like I can't protect you with this lifestyle. Every guy I see near you I think is another Jax. This shit was a mistake." He shook his head as he looked down at his sneakers. I knew he was just drunk and was overreacting, but so was I, and his words sliced through me. My chest felt like it had tightened, and I couldn't breathe.

"A mistake?" I could barely choke out the words. I couldn't believe he regretted being here with me. I pushed by him and rounded the table, needing to escape before my tears that threatened to fall spilled over. Everything had gone from great to shit in seconds. It didn't dawn on me until I reached the darkened parking lot—illuminated by a few sporadic streetlights—that I didn't have a place to call my own. Where was I even running to? I sighed heavily as I kicked at the loose gravel. It was time to be a grown-up and face my problems. I owed it to Tucker to hash this out and not just disappear.

"Hey," Tucker called from behind me. I spun around to face him as the door to the back entrance slammed closed. He shoved his hands into jean pockets as he slowly walked toward me. "I know you're pissed off at me for wanting to take care of you."

"What? You think that's why I'm mad? Tucker, you said this was a mistake. You called us a mistake." My voice wavered as a tear rolled down over my cheek.

"Jesus, Cass. I didn't mean us." He closed the space between us with two large strides, wrapping one arm behind my back and gripping the back of my head with his other hand. I squeezed my eyes closed, breathing in a deep lung full of his scent. "I could never regret this. You are *everything* to me."

"Then why did you say it?" I asked, looking up to him as I searched for the truth in his eyes.

"I meant coming on this tour. I should have just quit the fucking band like I had planned." His grip tightened around me.

"What do you mean you planned to leave the band?"

"I told the guys before I left to find you that if you didn't want to leave, I was going to stay with you. Even if you didn't want me. I was going to wait for you."

"Tucker. This band is your life."

"Not anymore." His mouth pressed against mine softly, and all of my anger and sadness evaporated with his touch. "I love you, Cass."

"I love you, too, Tucker."

"That's all I need, sweetheart."

"I think we should lay off on the drinking for the rest of the night," I joked, and he wrapped his arm over my shoulders and guided me toward the bus.

"I think you should have suggested that a half an hour ago." He laughed as he stumbled over his own feet. I placed my hand on his stomach to keep him steady.

As we approached the bus we heard a loud bang and what sounded like a growl. Our eyes met as we both looked at each other with confusion.

"What was that?" My feet froze to the ground.

"Wait here. I'll check it out." He waited for me to nod that I understood and wouldn't move. I bounced on my feet nervously as he walked away.

"Tucker!" I whispered loudly from behind him. He turned to look at me, his eyebrows pulled together. "Shouldn't we just get one of the guards or something?"

Another loud noise came from inside, and it sounded like a wounded animal.

"Fuck." Tucker ran his hand over his hair from back to front as he blew out a dramatic breath. "It's E."

"What is wrong with him?" My drunken memories grew

clearer, and I remembered the hurt in Eric's eyes as he saw Sarah dancing with Derek. "Great. This is my fault." I threw my hands in the air and walked around Tucker.

"Where do you think you're going?" he asked as he jogged to my side and gripped my elbow to stop me.

"I'm the one who upset him, now I'm going to fix it."

"This isn't your fault, Cass. This was Sarah. I told you how she was."

"She didn't do anything wrong. She just danced with a boy." I crossed my arms over my chest as I became defensive of my friend. "I'm the one who drew attention to it."

"Sarah and Eric were fuckups long before you came around. That ain't changing anytime soon."

"So what's the plan?" I asked, glancing to the bus.

"I'm going to go in and see if I can't get him to take his meds. You can wait by the door." He pressed a kiss into my hair and opened the door to the bus. I took a deep breath and stepped inside.

"Leave me the fuck alone!" Eric was sitting on Tucker's bunk with his legs on the floor. He was rocking with his hands holding his head.

"Cass, what are you doing in here?" Tucker turned to me. I held up my hands and shrugged. I should have stayed where he asked, but I wanted to help.

"Just fucking go!" Eric yelled, his voice strained. This was not the normal reaction to a broken heart.

"Calm down. We just want to talk to you." Tucker's tone was anything but sympathetic, and the last thing we needed was Eric turning his anger on him.

"Take your fairy tale happily ever after shit and get the fuck out of my face." Eric's eyes looked vacant.

"So what? No one can be happy if you're not?" Tucker yelled back, his arms spread out like he was inviting a fight.

"I don't think yelling at him is going to help anything," I yelled, and both guys looked at me, surprised by my outburst. "Give me a minute?"

Tucker looked from me to Eric, unsure if he wanted to leave me alone with him while he was upset. Judging by the broken stereo at Eric's feet, he had already gotten out most of his aggression.

"Five minutes and if I hear any yelling, I am coming in here and kicking his ass."

Eric snorted at the threat, and Tucker narrowed his eyes, not finding any of this amusing.

"Thank you." I gave Tucker a quick kiss on the cheek and waited for him to leave the bus. Eric stared at the broken and mangled plastic on the floor.

I wrung my fingers together as I stepped over the mess and took a seat on the bunk in front of him.

"I've actually been wanting to have a conversation with you, one-on-one."

Eric looked up at me and dropped his gaze to the floor.

"I don't want me being here to affect the band, and if that is the case, I'm happy to leave."

He didn't respond, so I continued to ramble nervously.

"You know, Sarah likes you. Things between her and Derek are complicated."

"I'm aware of her situation with Derek," he replied quietly.

"Maybe you could talk to him."

"I know you are trying to help, but I don't need it or want it. You have no idea what you're talking about."

This time I laughed.

"Which part don't I understand? The jealous ex-boyfriend? Uncontrollable anger and violent tendencies? Or being in love with someone you can't be with?"

He looked up again, nodding in understanding. There was a long pregnant pause as I pushed around a piece of the radio with my foot.

"She's perfect for me. She's funny and beautiful and she doesn't look at me like I'm some raging asshole."

"No one thinks you're an asshole."

He raised an eyebrow, and I giggled, nodding my head.

"Okay, that isn't entirely true, but they all love you. You wouldn't be a part of this band if they didn't."

"They won't if I keep doing shit like this."

"So stop."

"It's not that simple, Cass."

"Yes, it is. Do you want to lose everything? Your band? Your friends?"

"This band is my entire life."

"Then you need to act like it."

The door to the bus opened, and Tucker stepped inside, clearing his throat. I pushed up from the bunk and placed my hand on Eric's shoulder.

"Thank you," he said, and I could see in his eyes he was sincere. I smiled and made my way to the front of the bus.

CHAPTER

Ten

THE NEXT FEW weeks flew by as the guys played concert after concert. One show blurred into the next, every city looked the same, and my body was screaming for a break from the constant travel. I wouldn't change a thing though. After Eric and I talked, the band seemed to be growing closer, and I felt like I fit in with all of them. Sarah and I spent our free time shopping and just hanging out while the guys continued to work out the logistics of bringing a new manager on board. Sarah had confided in me that she and Derek were trying to work things out, and I was happy for her, but worried about how Eric would react when he found out.

"You think she's pretty?" Sarah doodled in her notebook as I tried to figure out the last line of my poem.

"Who?" I tapped my pen against my paper to the beat of my song. The guys had been practicing the song I wrote for weeks, and tonight they were finally going to play it in front of a crowd.

"This new manager chick. I bet she's a rock-star groupie."

"Come on. I'm sure she's just another Dorris."

"You're not the slightest bit worried?"

"Nope."

"You're a better woman than I am." She went back to doodling, and I glanced up at her, chewing on my lip. I hadn't given the new manager much thought, but now the seed of doubt had been planted. I already knew she wasn't thrilled about Tucker bringing his girlfriend on the road, but he assured me that he had made it clear I won't be going anywhere and that I was earning my keep with song lyrics.

"How bad could she be? It's not like the guys are going to put up with any bullshit. I trust their judgment." But I knew Tucker had major reservations about hiring her. If things started off rocky, I was going to grit my teeth and deal with it because I had pushed him to do what was best for the band, regardless of her opinion about me being on tour with them.

"You're probably right. What you and Tucker have doesn't come around often."

"Everything okay with you and Derek?" Sarah was being unusually negative.

She stopped drawing and sniffled.

"What's going on? You know you can talk to me." It felt

good to be a friend to someone. Sarah had been a tremendous help as I adjusted to this new lifestyle.

"He's been really distant, and I know our on again–off again relationship has been hell on the band. If I have to choose between him and our future, I feel like I have to follow my dreams."

"I'm so sorry, Sarah."

"We should get ready. I have to rehearse soon."

I nodded, and we didn't speak anymore about her relationship falling apart. I could tell there was more going on than what she was saying, but she wasn't ready to share it, so I didn't push. I knew how that felt.

I grabbed my new bag of makeup from under the bathroom sink, and we got to work on getting ourselves concert ready. I was warming up to doing all of the girly rituals that I had avoided for most of my life. It felt good to take care of myself, to try to look my best. Sarah painted herself in heavy black eyeliner and dark lipstick, while I made myself look natural and fresh faced. Our styles were polar opposites, but I couldn't imagine finding a better friend or confidante in anyone else.

"You want to borrow one of my dresses?" she asked as she shook out her hair. I rolled my eyes and carefully applied clear lip gloss to my mouth.

"Tucker would have a fit. You remember the little black dress incident." I laughed.

"You looked hot, and from what I remember he couldn't keep his hands off you." She cocked an eyebrow at my reflection in the mirror of the tiny bathroom.

"Neither could that pervert at the after-party." I ran my fingers through my hair, pulling it over my shoulder as I inspected my face.

"So now you dress according to how some loser acts? Tucker is a great guy, but it isn't his decision, and it's not his job to protect you from the world. You're a big girl. You can take care of yourself."

My memories flashed to Jax and my inability to stand up for myself with him. If it hadn't been for Tucker, I probably wouldn't have survived that last night with him. But that threat was long gone, and I couldn't continue to live my life being worried about the rest of the world.

"What did you have in mind?"

"Really?" She practically squealed as she pulled me from the bathroom and we made our way to her bus to find something to wear. I loved dressing up more than I let on. It reminded me of the day Tucker took me to Scarlett's and bought me that beautiful dress, our first unofficial date. It was the first time in a very long time that I had felt beautiful. I had closed myself off to people, but that night Tucker had convinced me to dance with him and I enjoyed myself more than I had in years.

After a half an hour of rummaging through her mountain

of clothing, we decided on a sweet little flowy black skirt and matching black T-shirt that was skintight and revealed a tiny sliver of skin at the waist. Sarah changed into head-to-toe black as well, but she completed her look with ripped black fishnet stockings and army boots.

"What do you think?" she asked, spinning around.

"You look like a rock star."

"That was the goal." She laughed.

Sarah took off for practice, and I decided to take a walk and get to see some of North Carolina before we were off to another state. As much as we traveled, I rarely saw anything outside of the bus. The weather was perfect, not too hot or too cold. The area had a very small-town feel to it with rolling pastures, and it made me miss home for the first time since I had left to go on tour with Tucker.

I only made it a few blocks before the familiar sound of Tucker's bike approached me from behind. He pulled off the side of the road and took off his helmet, running his hand through his messy hair.

"What brings you out here all by yourself?" he asked, and I turned to face him, shielding my eyes from the bright sun.

"Taking in the scenery."

He knocked down the kickstand with his boot and leaned his bike onto it, standing and stretching as his eyes scanned the fields.

"Mind if I join you?"

"Of course not." I gave him a smile and held out my hand for him. He wrapped his fingers around mine, and we began to walk slowly through the grass. "You look amazing, by the way."

I couldn't help but grin at his compliment.

"I was worried you wouldn't like it."

"How could I not like it?" He bumped me with his shoulder playfully.

"After the pervert at the after-party . . ." I let my voice trail off as Tucker stopped walking and turned to face me.

"I was upset. No one likes to have some asshole putting his hands all over his girlfriend, but I overreacted about the dress. It wasn't your fault, and if I made you feel like that was somehow your fault . . . well, I'm sorry."

I leaned in, placing a soft kiss on his lips, my eyes falling closed. His hand pushed against the small of my back, pulling my body closer to his.

"I've been stressing a lot lately with the tour and new manager, and it isn't fair to take that shit out on you."

"I think we could both use a little break from all of this craziness," I said as I took a step back from his arms. His eyebrows pulled together in worry as he tried to figure out where I was going with this.

I fumbled with the hem of my shirt before I took in a quick, deep breath and tugged it over my head and let it fall to the ground beside me. Tucker stepped forward, his fingers tangling in my hair as he pressed his mouth against mine hard. I let my lips part as I slipped my fingers under the edge of his shirt, running them over the ridges of his stomach. He groaned and released my hair, yanking his shirt over his head before his body was back against mine like a magnet.

"You sure about this?" he mumbled against my lips. I grabbed the button of his jeans, letting him know I wasn't going to change my mind. His hand slid up my side, and his fingers traced the delicate fabric of my bra.

I was tired of worrying, and I needed to get lost in the moment, needed to forget our past. Tucker slowly lowered me to the grass, his fingers brushing the hair from my forehead as he stared into my eyes.

"I love you, Cass. I know things have been difficult with all that is going on, but I don't want you to do something you aren't ready for. We have forever, sweetheart. I promise."

"I love you, Tucker." I closed my eyes, smiling like a fool as the sunshine warmed my face. He rolled beside me, taking my hand in his.

"When all this is over, I want a big yard like this. No people for miles. Just us," he said.

"I never want to leave this place," I whispered. His fingers squeezed mine and my heart sank. "We should make the time worthwhile." I grinned as I raised up on my elbow beside him. I leaned over and gave him a kiss, coaxing his lips open with my tongue. He groaned again, his arms circling my waist and pulling me down on him. I straddled his body as one of his hands slid up my side and tangled in my hair. The other gripped onto my butt and held me tight against his body. I slowly rocked my hips against his, and he let out a small moan in the back of his throat as he deepened our kiss. I missed having time alone with Tucker. We needed more of it to grow as a couple, but I was willing to take any opportunity I could get. My hands slid over his toned chest. I could feel his heartbeat pounding back against my fingertips. I loved that even with thousands of girls screaming his name at his concerts, I was still able to make him feel excited. It was empowering. His hips began to move with mine, his jeans rubbing hard against me. I panted into his mouth, getting lost in how amazing his touch felt. His lips left mine as he kissed a trail over my jaw to my throat. His fingers slid over my shoulder. He pushed the cup of my bra below my breast as his thumb, calloused from playing his guitar, ran over my nipple, causing it to pebble under his touch.

"If we don't stop now, I won't be able to." His words sent a burst of heat radiating through my core. I didn't want him to stop, but I didn't want our first time of making love since we got back together to be in a field. I reluctantly sat up, struggling to catch my breath as I pulled my bra back into place.

"We should go." I slid off Tucker and grabbed my shirt, pulling it down over my head. Tucker sat beside me, reaching over and pulling a piece of grass from my hair and tossing it aside.

The ride back was short, but I forgot how much I loved being on the back of Tucker's bike. It felt good to hang on to him and just escape. I wished we had more moments like this.

When we got back to the bus, we didn't have much time before the concert, and I was incredibly excited to hear my words being sung onstage to thousands of people. Tucker had been working on it for a few days and had yet to let me hear him sing it. I was nervous to hear my words coming from his mouth, in front of thousands of people, no less. I was practically bouncing off the walls. Backstage, Eric questioned whether I was on drugs. I laughed and told him that for the first time in a long time, I was just high on life.

"I feel like I am finally figuring out who I want to be," I said.

"I'm glad. I was worried how this whole tour thing would work out," Tucker said.

I wrapped my arms around Tucker's waist and squeezed him.

"Nothing worthwhile is ever easy," I said.

"That's good. You should put that in your next song." He smiled down at me. We stared at each other for a long moment before his smile faded and his body tensed under my arms.

"What is it?" I pulled back slightly to get a better look at his face.

"We're gonna meet up with Donna after the show. She will be stopping by to check out the bus and get ready to move in."

"I don't understand why she would want to live on a bus with a bunch of crazy rock stars."

"Hey . . . you live with a bunch of crazy rock stars."

"Yeah, but that is because I am in love with one of them. I bet she doesn't last a week with you guys."

"It's not the guys I'm worried about." He raised an eyebrow.

"I'm excited to have another girl around. It's her that wishes otherwise."

"She will love you. How could she not? She just needs to get to know you."

"We're on," Terry called from behind us, and I frowned, hating how little time I got to actually spend with my boyfriend even though we were living together.

"Good luck." I gave Tucker a kiss on the cheek, and he playfully patted my butt before following after his other bandmates. I made my way over to the refreshment table and grabbed a soda, popping it open and taking a large gulp. My nerves were taking over, and suddenly I wanted to disappear. I was terrified that the crowd would hate my song, that it wouldn't feel like a genuine Damaged song. I wanted to run back out to the bus and hide in our bunk.

"They're starting." Sarah laughed, pointing back to the stage. She was covered in a thin layer of sweat and looked as if she was glowing.

"I'm heading out there, just taking a break."

"Are you scared?" She walked over to me and grabbed my drink, guzzling it down before tossing it in the trash a few feet away.

"I don't know how you do it. You get up on a stage in front of thousands and just pour your heart out. What if they don't like you?"

"Fuck what they think. This is about doing what I love, following my dreams. If they like it, that's just icing on the cake. If I lived my life worried about everyone else, I would go insane." She laughed, and I shook my head.

"You are wise beyond your years," I joked, and Sarah got a faraway look in her eyes.

"Let's go watch *your* dreams come true." She grabbed my arm and pulled me to the stage.

The crowd was going wild for Tucker as usual. He began with an old favorite, "Loved." I hummed along and got lost in the lyrics as he smiled down at his adoring fans who reached out to him, even though they were nowhere near close enough to touch him. He was a sexy rock god, and he was mine.

"What are you grinning about?" Sarah nudged me with her elbow as she laughed.

"I'm just . . . happy. It feels nice."

"I'm happy for you." She grinned. Tucker sat down on a stool in the center of the stage as the lights dimmed and a spotlight shined on him. He adjusted the mic and began to play the first few chords of "Empty Sheets," my song. I froze, my heart racing in my chest as the crowd fell silent and he began to sing. His eyes closed and I held my breath as he sang the first lyric. It was the most beautiful thing I'd ever heard, and my chest swelled with pride at the thought of us making such beautiful music together. My gaze fluttered over the crowd at the women who held their hands to their chests and swayed. Some openly cried as the emotions overtook them, others clung to their significant others in a tight embrace. It was surreal to see so many taking my words to heart, and as Tucker glanced in my direction, everyone else faded away.

The world was ours, and I looked up at the man I loved as he poured as much of his own heart into the song singing it as I had while writing it. I could feel him pouring his emotions into my words, and I was moved by the way he connected with them, with me.

"I love you," I mouthed, and his lips quirked up in a grin before singing the next line. Everything fell into place in that moment. The past, the struggles, the fears all evaporated, and I felt like I belonged, like I had a purpose.

As the song ended and Tucker strummed his guitar one last time, the crowd erupted into cheers. Happy tears spilled onto my cheek as I clapped along with them. Tucker stood, smiling as he leaned over the mic.

"I love you, too." He shot me a wink, and my heart melted.

It didn't matter that thousands of women thought he was professing his love to them; I knew he was speaking only to me.

It was surreal seeing something I had created with the painful memories of my past be turned into something beautiful, and having Tucker help me through it made it a bonding experience for us.

CHAPTER

Eleven

I SLEPT LIKE A rock the night after the show and was barely able to pull myself out of our cramped bunk by noon the next day. Keeping up with the schedule was torture on my body, and I was beginning to feel like an old lady.

I got myself ready for the day fairly quickly and sat around for the next hour trying to think up lyrics to a new song, but my mind was blank. The guys were off meeting with their new manager, and I didn't expect them back anytime soon, so I decided to clean the bus. It only took me three hours to get it sparkling, and I had worked up a major appetite. I decided I would whip up a nice dinner. I had bought a few boxes of stuffing mix and instant mashed potatoes. It was the closest you could get to a home-cooked meal when you had only a microwave at your disposal, and I wanted the new manager to feel welcome.

I heard Tucker's bike approach, and I jumped up to look out the small window by the kitchen table. He was being followed by a large SUV. I smoothed my hair and bounded out of the bus to greet them.

"Cass, this is Donna, the new manager. Donna, this is my girlfriend, Cass." I looked over the woman in her pencil skirt and button-down white-collared shirt.

"Nice to meet you." I gave her my biggest smile. She was incredibly attractive, standing about half a foot taller than I did with long, wavy, dark-brown hair that she kept pinned back on the sides. Her eyes were the brightest green I had ever seen—they had to be contacts.

"Likewise," she replied as her eyes danced over the bus.

"Come on in. I was just getting ready to make dinner." I smiled at Tucker, and he cleared his throat.

"Actually, were going out for dinner." He gave me an apologetic shrug.

"Oh." I smiled at how adorable he was when he didn't want to disappoint me. "No problem. Let me grab my shoes and we can head out."

"This is a business meeting, dear," Donna cut in. I looked to Tucker, but he was staring at his feet, clearly trying to sidestep the awkwardness inherent in the situation at hand.

"That's fine. I'll just have dinner with Filth. Those boys have been looking a little skinny lately." I maintained my smile, struggling to keep from looking like my feelings were hurt. I knew things would change when Donna arrived, I just didn't realize that it would happen so quickly. I hoped that things would smooth out quickly.

"I can bring you something back if you want?" Tucker's hand grabbed my side as his thumb rubbed small circles over my hip.

"No, it's fine. Don't be silly. Have fun." I leaned forward and gave him a kiss on the lips, feeling awkward with this stranger watching us.

"I won't be long. I promise." He shot me a wink. The rest of the band didn't say a word, and I suddenly felt like an outsider in our odd little family.

I slinked back inside our bus feeling sorry for myself. Things were going to change, and I hoped it would be for the better. The band needed someone to look out for them and their best interest, and Donna promised to be the professional who could take them to the next level. Still, I had a terrible feeling in my gut that this would put a strain on my relationship with the guys . . . and with Tucker.

I grabbed my notebook and began to pour out my feelings, holding nothing back. There was a small knock on the bus door before it pulled open, and Sarah stepped inside. I glanced up at her and went back to my writing.

"I saw the guys leave with that evil-looking secretary," she said as she slid into the seat across from me.

"That's the new manager, Donna." I sighed and began to

doodle on the edge of the notebook paper. "They went out for dinner."

"Why didn't you go along? Not feeling well?"

"I'm not a part of the band," I replied, and I felt like an idiot for even being upset. I wasn't a member of the band, and I really had no business at the meeting.

"Come on. You write their songs, keep them fed, and stop Eric from having a meltdown every other day. I'd say you have a very important role in this band."

"It's no big deal. Really. I needed to write more anyway."

Sarah grabbed my notebook and turned it around so she could read what I had written. She smiled and slid it back over to me.

"I need to hire you to write for us. This is really good."

I rolled my eyes and flipped the cover closed.

"Let's go eat something."

I sighed dramatically but was thankful I had made a friend that cared about my happiness. It felt good to know I could count on someone.

We opted for fast food to minimize the chances of running into the band while we were out. I didn't want to interrupt whatever they had to discuss.

I ordered the biggest burger I could find, and Sarah got a salad, claiming she had to watch what she ate or risk not fitting into her tour wardrobe, even though she was built like a model.

"So tell me your backstory," she said between bites.

I had absolutely no idea where to begin. So I started with the basics, deciding to gauge her reaction as I went before I revealed the really heavy stuff.

"I lived in a really small town in Georgia."

"Do you miss it?"

"Not really." That wasn't true. I loved being with Tucker, but when I lived on my own, I had finally been able to rely on myself, and that had felt really good. I felt like an adult for the first time in my life. Now I was just along for the ride to someone else's dreams.

"Family?"

"None that I know." My father was the only family I had left, but I wasn't even certain he was still alive. "You?"

"Mom and Dad don't want anything to do with me and my devil music." She rolled her eyes and chuckled, but I knew it bothered her more than she let on.

"Siblings?" I took another huge bite of my burger, savoring the greasy mess.

"I have a little sister. She's really cool. Looks just like me with lighter hair. I miss her."

"I'm an only child." I shrugged. "I always wished I had a sister, but it is probably better I don't."

She pulled her eyebrows together as she took a sip of her drink. "Why do you say that? You fight all the time, but no one has your back like a sister or brother."

"It was a bad situation." I couldn't imagine having to take care of a child in the situation I was in. Not to mention having another mouth to feed, another person to protect from Jax's fists and my mom's needles.

"Well, you have me now." She grinned and I smiled back. She was starting to feel more like family to me than my own mother ever had.

We headed back to the bus, and I noticed movement through the windows. Sarah gave me a sympathetic look and I waved her on.

"It'll be fine. I can handle one bitch. I used to waitress."

"I'll see you at the show then," she called out as she circled around the bus.

I took a deep breath and pulled open the door. Eric was rambling a mile a minute about how much he hated when fans threw themselves at him, and I worried that something happened during their meal, but Tucker looked un-phased.

"Where you been, sweetheart?" he asked with a grin. I walked over to him, kissing him on the cheek. Donna was nowhere in sight. I relaxed into his arms.

"Went out with Sarah for some food."

Eric slammed a cabinet door and I jumped.

"What's up with him?" I asked as I watched him storm around like an animal.

"Some guy was hounding him and put him in one of his moods." Tucker rolled his eyes.

"Want me to talk to him?"

"Be my guest." He shrugged and let his hands fall to his sides.

"Eric," I called out to him, and he turned to face me, his eyes void of anything. "Can I talk to you outside?" I asked, and he looked around before finally nodding and walking out the door, letting it bounce off the outside of the bus. Tucker shot me a worried look, but I wasn't going to let him talk me out of helping Eric.

"Love you." I gave Tucker a quick peck on the cheek and followed after Eric.

He was leaning up against the side of the bus, staring off at the buildings that lined the other side of the parking lot.

"One of those days, right?" I said, and he didn't acknowledge me. "Sarah and I were talking about our families today." He glanced my way at the mention of her name. I kept talking, knowing that if we spoke long enough he would forget what had upset him.

"She has a little sister. Did you know that? I'm an only child."

"I had a little brother," he said quietly. I wasn't sure if I should ask what happened. I didn't know if it would help him to talk about it or send him deeper into his funk.

"Hit by a fucking car." He shook his head and looked down to the ground. "Nine years old, not even old enough to drive, and he gets taken out by a fucking car."

"I'm so sorry."

His eyes cut to mine and narrowed.

"Why are you sorry? You drive the car?"

"No." I shrugged.

"Then you got no reason to be sorry."

"I'm sorry that it happened . . . and I'm sorry that I brought it up," I said honestly.

"Don't be. No one wants to talk to me about him. But honestly, I like to think about him. I like to remember." He rubbed his hand roughly over the back of his neck. "But you know what it's like." His eyes met mine again, and I knew he felt a kinship because of all the people I had lost. I nodded, my throat closing up.

"I'm not sure I would want to talk about those sort of things."

"You don't know until you try."

I nodded but still wasn't sure I was ready.

"You just gotta know it's not your fault." He gazed off into the distance. I didn't know if he was speaking to himself or to me. "It took me years to not blame myself. I was right there. I could have shoved him out of the way. I could have done something, but I froze. I just stood there as the car drove off the road into our front yard. I couldn't even scream."

"I, uh . . . I let my mom get killed by my boyfriend . . . who also tried to kill me, but only managed to . . . kill my baby. Some days I wish he had been more successful." I was surprised at how easily the honesty poured out of me. It was freeing, like opening up a gate to my soul.

Eric walked over to me and placed his hand on my shoulder.

"I know I'm not easy to get along with, and maybe that's because I think no one gets it, the survivor's guilt, I guess." He sighed, and I could see him contemplating what to say next. "But you get it. Thank you."

I nodded, swallowing hard. That confession had drained the energy from me.

"For what it's worth, I'm glad you're still here." He gave me a small smile and stepped back onto the bus.

CHAPTER

Twelve

THE DAYS BLED together into one endless string of concerts and driving occasionally punctuated by an argument with Donna. She was determined to get me off the bus, and I was hell-bent on standing my ground. It was easy to forget there was more going on in the world than what was happening with the band.

"This band is awesome," the guy on the other side of the guardrail yelled to me as the next concert got under way. He didn't look like your typical rock-concert goer. He was wearing jeans and a button-up plaid shirt that hung open over a white cotton tee. A giant camera hung from his neck.

"Yeah, they're great." I kept my eyes fixed on the stage as Tucker belted out the chorus to "Empty Sheets." "Are you a photographer?" I asked, motioning to the camera.

"Oh, this?" He picked up the camera and turned it over in his hand. "Just a hobby. This song is amazing!"

I couldn't help but smile. "Tucker can make anything sound good," I replied.

"You know him? Like friends with him?" he asked, and the question made me feel uncomfortable. "I guess that's why you get to stand on *that* side of the railing."

"He's my boyfriend." I knew I was blushing, but I couldn't help it. I relished the rare moments when I got to break the rules a bit and talk about my relationship with someone.

"That's got to be crazy. I bet it's hard going so long without seeing each other."

"I travel with him." I grinned and listened to the band begin their next song.

"That's pretty cool."

The music picked up, putting an end to the chitchat. I loved watching Tucker perform. It never got old watching him do what he loved. I hoped one day I would be as satisfied in whatever I chose to do with my life.

After his set ended I slipped backstage and waited for him just out of sight of the concertgoers. I wrapped my arms around his neck and kissed him as he lifted my feet from the ground.

"You're sweaty." I made a face, and he sat me back on my feet and grinned.

"Want to get sweaty with me?" He cocked his eyebrow.

"Mmmm . . ." I pretended to think about it, and Tucker

picked me up as I wrapped my legs around his waist, giggling. He pressed my back against the cinder-block wall and kissed me. There was nothing playful about his kiss. His tongue slid over my lower lip and I let my mouth fall open, inviting him inside.

"They're asking for you," Chris called out from the door.

"Fuck." Tucker rested his forehead against mine and closed his eyes. "I have to go sign some autographs, and we have that VIP thing tonight."

I nodded as I dropped my legs and he lowered me to the ground. I was beginning to wonder if the timing would ever be right for me and Tucker again. I was finally feeling like I could push away the past and get lost in the kisses of my boyfriend . . . and now he had to go. Again.

"It's fine. I'll go hang out on the bus." I gave him a quick kiss on the nose and waited for him to walk back out toward the stage. With a sigh I retreated back to the bus to spend the next few hours by myself. I hated being alone, but it gave me time to write and it had become a great way for me to work through everything I was still carrying around with me.

I made my way out of the back exit of the building and slipped into the bus that was parked just behind the doors. Tonight we had security posted outside, and it made me nervous to think how things were changing so rapidly.

I grabbed my notebook and began to jot down lines as they floated through my head. Nothing was really coming together, but Tucker had told me that when he writes it never seems to make sense at first, so I didn't let it discourage me. After a good two hours of getting lost in my memories, I knew it was going to be a long night for the guys, and it was no use waiting up. I crawled into bed alone and stared at the pictures of Tucker taped overhead before drifting off to sleep.

CHAPTER

Thirteen

*D*ON'T FREAK OUT." Sarah put her hand on my chest and stopped me from entering the checkout at the grocery store.

"Okay, Sarah, you can't grab my boobs and ask me not to freak out. That's just weird."

"What? No!" She pulled her hand back and grabbed a tabloid magazine from the end of the counter. "This!" She pointed to a giant picture of my face.

"What?" I snatched the magazine from her hand, turning it over several times like the image would disappear. "This is bad. This is so bad."

"It might be. See what it says." She grabbed another magazine from the rack and flipped it open to the article.

"I didn't do an interview. How do they have this?" I asked, pointing to the quotes directly from me. It finally dawned on me. . . . The man at the Damaged concert back in Lakeland. The guy with the camera. "Shit. That weird guy from the concert. I didn't know he was a reporter. They can't do this without permission, right?" I asked. Nothing in the story was actually that bad. It mentioned that I was Tucker's girlfriend and that I was touring with him. That didn't seem so terrible.

"We should let them see this before they find it on their own . . . or before Donna finds it." Sarah grabbed the rest of the magazines, and we checked out as quickly as possible. I didn't see why it was such a big deal. In fact, I was certain Tucker would get a laugh out of it. I knew he wasn't a fan of these magazines, but this story happened to be true this time.

I slipped onto the bus, and the guys were going about their morning routines, which consisted of nursing their hangovers and Chris very unceremoniously kicking his one-night stand off the bus.

"Breaking Donna's rules?" I raised an eyebrow at Chris who shook his head with a guilty grin. "She's out getting her fancy coffee or some shit."

I shook my head and sat my bags of groceries on the floor, pulling out the contents and slipping them into the cupboards. Tucker came out of the bathroom, his hair an adorable mess and his basketball shorts slung low on his hips.

"Morning, sweetheart," he said as he gave me a kiss on the cheek and started helping me unload the groceries. He pulled out a magazine, and his eyes grew large as he looked at my face on the cover. "What the hell is this?"

"Don't be mad. Some guy was talking to me at your concert. I had no idea who he was."

Tucker flipped through the pages and glanced over the interview.

"Why would I be mad?" He slowly ripped the cover off the magazine and dug through the kitchen drawer, pulling out a roll of tape. "I like this picture of you." He smiled and went back to his bunk to tape the picture above his bed with the others. I sighed, thankful he didn't react the way Sarah had feared.

"You guys hungry?" I asked as Eric grabbed a coffee mug from the sink.

"Coffee?" He held the cup out at me with the saddest little puppy-dog face.

"I'll get right on it." I took the mug and sat it on the counter. He gave me a thankful smile, and I began preparing the coffeemaker for a fresh pot. The door opened and Donna stepped inside holding a drink carrier full of overpriced lattes. She sat it down on the table and pulled off her oversized sunglasses. Her eyes landed on me and narrowed before she dug around in her giant hobo purse and pulled out a copy of the magazine with my article. She held it up, not saying a word. I turned back to the coffeemaker and continued to fill it with water.

"I've already seen it," I said, not looking at her. "So has Tucker."

"It's a great picture," Tucker spoke up, sliding his hand around my back and resting his hand on my hip.

"So I guess it was worth losing half of your fan base?" Donna shot back. I spun around. "We had discussed this, Tucker." Her eyes narrowed and landed on my boyfriend.

"Discussed what?" I asked, looking to him for answers. He blew out a long breath.

"Donna thinks we should keep our relationship a secret. She's afraid our female fans will lose interest."

"Not a secret. I think it shouldn't exist."

"What?" I knew she had reservations about me joining the guys for the tour, but this was insane.

"It's nothing personal."

"Nothing personal? This is my boyfriend. I don't see how it could be any more personal."

She turned her attention to Tucker, completely ignoring me.

"I have been fielding calls all morning. Calls from everyone from news reporters to Cass's father and everyone in between. This is very bad."

"Wait . . . Did you say my father?" Suddenly I felt like I was spinning. . . . In that one sentence the entire world just imploded.

"This isn't a game, Tucker. Is it really worth it to play house with some girl? This is your career."

"She isn't just some girl. I love her, and she is more important than any of this shit."

"I'm sorry. Did you say my dad called you?"

Donna rolled her eyes at me as she tapped her foot. The other members of the band stood in shock watching our fight. Tucker continued to argue his point while Donna shrieked and moaned.

"Enough," Eric yelled, and the bus went silent. I leaned back against the counter, struggling to catch my breath as a panic attack began to take over. "Cass is trying to find out about her dad. Can you not see what you're doing to her?" Suddenly everyone's eyes were on me.

"He left his number. Why is this such a big issue?" Donna waved her hands around dramatically. I slowly raised my eyes to meet hers.

"I haven't seen my father in years. . . . Since I was little," I said quietly as I rubbed over my arm nervously. I hated admitting that I fit the stereotype she had clearly pinned on me: poor little lost girl with daddy issues. I expected her to smile, but instead she was sympathetic.

"That wasn't fair of me. I didn't know."

"It's fine," I said, looking away. I needed to get out of there. I needed some air before my lungs exploded. I pushed my way through the group and stumbled out of the front door. Tucker followed and placed his hand on the small of my back.

"I'm sorry. I didn't think."

I held up my hand to stop him from talking. I knew he wasn't trying to hurt me, but all I cared about in that moment was keeping the world from caving in on me. My father had disappeared to New Orleans when I was six and never returned, leaving my mother and me destitute and confused, struggling to survive while he was off living the single life. What could he possibly want from me now, so many years later?

I shook away the sadness, forcing back the tears that threatened to spill over my cheeks. "I always knew he would come back one day; I just thought it would be while my mother was still alive." My heart was in the pit of my stomach. Tucker wrapped his arms around me, and that contact, that feeling of safety, caused me to let go of everything I was holding back. The tears flowed freely as sobs wracked my body. This wasn't supposed to happen. I was happy now, and my life was finally falling into place.

Tucker laid his cheek on the top of my head as his hand rubbed over my back soothingly.

"This doesn't change anything. You don't have to call him back. He doesn't deserve it."

I pulled back, brushing my hair away from my wet face.

"I have to call him, Tucker. He's my dad." I couldn't understand his logic. Why would I blow him off? I had wanted to see his face again since the moment he stepped out of my life.

"You don't have to do anything, Cass. He doesn't even deserve to hear your voice. You're going to get hurt."

"I'm used to it." I walked around him and made my way around the bus. I wanted to talk to Sarah. She would understand. I knew Tucker didn't want to see me upset, but that was something in life that was unavoidable. I was willing to take the chance.

I banged on the bus door and waited impatiently for someone to answer. Derek pulled open the door and motioned with a tilt of his head to the back of the bus. Sarah leaned out of the bathroom where she was styling her hair to see who was at the door.

"Hey! I was gonna come get you in a few and see if you wanted to do makeovers." She was beaming from ear to ear. Her smile faded as she saw my tearstained face. "What's wrong?"

"Nothing." I swiped the tears from my cheeks and gave her a smile. "I was just overwhelmed."

She made her way down the hallway of the bus. Derek gave her a look and nodded, going to the back of the bus to give us privacy. I shoved my hands in my jean pockets.

"How are things going with him?" I asked as she motioned for us to sit at the small kitchen table.

"Things are good. You want to tell me what happened? Is it Tucker? Is it that bitch Donna?"

I laughed and shook my head.

"Not really. I mean . . . yeah, she sucks, but it's not them."

"Then what is it? Spit it out already!"

"My dad is trying to contact me."

Sarah sat back in her seat, her eyes going wide.

"I take it that's a bad thing."

"No. I mean . . . I don't really know. I've been dreaming of this day for years."

She nodded and reached over the table, placing her hand on mine. Half her hair was curled, the other side hung in a tangled mess. I laughed.

"You have the power here. You don't have to see him if you don't want to. You can call and see where it goes from there. Just be careful. There is no telling what he wants."

"I know." The thought of him wanting something from me tied my stomach in knots. I wasn't ready to be hurt by someone else I loved, but I needed to hear his voice.

There was a knock on the door and Sarah grinned.

"Come in, Tucker," she called out, and the door pulled open. Tucker smiled when his eyes met mine.

"I guess I should go and let you finish getting ready." I pushed up from the table and walked toward the door.

"I'm here if you need to talk," Sarah replied as we made our way back outside.

"Tucker." I turned to face him, taking his hands in mine. "I need you to be supportive, no matter what I decide to do."

He nodded, looking down at the asphalt.

"If he hurts you . . ." His eyes met mine and I sighed, not needing him to finish his thought. He pulled a small slip of paper from his pocket and held it out to me. I took it from him. My eyes danced over the phone number scrawled out in Tucker's handwriting. I looped my arms around his neck and kissed his cheek as I gave him an appreciative hug.

"Thank you."

"Don't thank me yet. I'm not sure this is going to end the way you are hoping."

"When did you become so pessimistic?"

He laughed sardonically and ran his hand over his hair.

"When I lost everything I had loved."

The pain in his eyes nearly killed me. I pushed my forehead against his.

"I'm not going anywhere, Tucker." I pressed my lips against his, and he slid his hands into my hair, holding me against him for an extra moment.

"Just promise me, no matter what happens, you won't let him break you. You're a lot stronger than I give you credit for, but I have seen you defeated, and I don't ever want to watch you go through that again."

"No matter what happens, we have each other, and that is all I need."

"Band meeting." Donna stuck her head out of the door. I rolled my eyes and looked back at Tucker.

"At least you won't have to deal with her for a little while."

I laughed and pulled him in for a hug. He kissed my forehead and retreated back inside of the bus. A few minutes later the band filed out with Donna behind them.

I went onto the bus and sat down. I held the cell phone in my hands, letting my eyes go unfocused as I stared at the keypad. I was trying to summon the courage to finally call my dad. My fingers shook as I pulled the small sliver of paper from my pocket. This was it. Time to be strong. I dialed the number and dropped the paper in my lap as I crossed my legs in our bunk.

It rang twice before a man with a deep scratchy voice answered.

"Yeah?"

The voice didn't sound like I had remembered, and for a second I thought I had dialed the wrong number.

"I'm sorry, I was looking for David Daniels."

"This is him," he replied, and the line went quiet. "Cass?"

My throat closed and I suddenly was unable to respond. It was my father and he recognized me.

"It's me." I cleared my throat as I pushed open the curtain to the bunk, feeling claustrophobic.

"Princess! You sound so grown up."

"I am grown up now, Dad."

"Yeah, of course you are. Of course. How are you?"

"I'm . . . all right."

"Good. That's really good to hear. I tried to call your mother a few times, but she must have changed her number."

"She's dead," I blurted out, squeezing my eyes closed as I mentally scolded myself for not being more tactful. He didn't respond, but I could hear him breathing into the receiver. "I'm sorry. I didn't mean to tell you that way. I thought you would know."

There was a beat of silence.

"No, no, it's fine. I just . . . I . . . I didn't know."

"How are you doing?" I wanted to change the subject and not let myself dwell on the darker part of my life.

"Things are good. My wife is pregnant again."

Everything began to spin, and I felt like I was sinking.

"Your wife?" I asked as I held the palm of my hand against my chest. Willing my heartbeat to slow.

"I remarried a few years back. Your momma didn't tell you?"

"How could you remarry? You and Mom were still married." I was angry and wanted to scream at him in her defense.

"We've been divorced for nearly four years, Cass."

"That's impossible. You said she is pregnant *again*?"

"Big as a house. . . . You have a little brother, Ryley. He just turned three, but that boy is smart as a whip."

I let the phone slide from my hand and into my lap as I struggled to keep from losing my mind. All these years I had prayed for my father to come back and save us, and all the while he had moved on and started a whole new family. We couldn't have been further from his mind. And worst of all, Momma had known and never said a word. I felt betrayed by everyone involved. I could hear the faint sound of his voice from the phone, and I picked it up and held it back to my ear.

"Sorry. I dropped the phone." My voice came out sounding monotone. I was trying so hard to suppress the sadness and anger that was boiling inside of me.

"I thought she would have told you, princess."

"Why didn't *you* tell me?" I asked, surprised at my own strength.

"When I left I had no business trying to raise a kid when I couldn't even pay the bills. Couldn't even keep myself off the bottle. You were better off with your mother. I always planned to come back. You have to believe that, but your momma and I were toxic together. It would have made your life miserable."

"My life *was* miserable. We struggled every damn day." The tears were flowing freely now, and I was embarrassed that I was allowing him to hear me cry.

"I'm sorry. I know I can't ever take back what I have put you through, but I would like the chance to be a part of your life, Cass. Everyone deserves a second chance."

"But . . . why now?"

"When I saw your face on the magazine, it was a real wake-up call, Cass. . . . It was a punch in the gut. I realized how much time had passed . . . how much of your life I'd missed out on. . . . Hell, it took me a few moments to even recognize my own kid!" He laughed nervously, and then fell silent for a few moments. "I just want a second shot with my oldest kid, Cass. That's all."

I chewed on my lip as I thought that over. I knew people

could change, and he was taking the step to have me back in his life. That had to count for something.

"Okay," I replied with a sigh.

"Great. I'll call you to make some plans. Thank you, Cass."

I nodded to myself and ended the call, tossing the phone on the bed beside me as I tried to process all of the new information. I couldn't believe he had a new family and that it took him almost two decades to reach out to me. I could feel anger beginning to swell, but I fought against it. After all, it would be nice to have family. And he was all I had left.

I let the tears flow freely as I put my head on Tucker's pillow. I closed my eyes, inhaling the traces of coconut that lingered from him. His concert would be beginning soon, but my body felt like it weighed a thousand pounds and I couldn't force myself to move. I needed a night off. A break from all of the chaos that was life on the road.

I tried to imagine what my father's house would look like and if his son and I shared any resemblance. I always took after my mother, so the chances of that were pretty slim. Then my mind wandered to what his wife was like. Was she kind? Did she have any of the emotional issues that plagued my mother? I couldn't imagine that she would, as most of her problems seemed to stem from his abandonment of her, of us.

I hadn't even thought to ask him if he was still in New Orleans or if that was just another part of the fairy tale my parents fed me when I was little. I didn't know what to believe anymore. All I knew was I wasn't satisfied with what-ifs anymore. I needed to see him face-to-face.

My head was clouded with a mix of sadness and hope as I drifted off to sleep, exhausted from all of the emotions that were overwhelming me. I dreamt of my father. He looked as I remembered him but his features blurred slightly; I couldn't bring him into focus. His hair was peppered with gray, and he opened his arms to me with a bright smile. I ran to him and was immediately swarmed by my new loving family. They gripped me tightly in their arms and all had the same comforting beachy smell.

"I missed you tonight." A voice spoke to me, and I laughed at how much my father sounded like Tucker. "You feeling okay?"

My eyes fluttered open and I was face-to-face with Tucker who had curled up beside me in the bunk.

"I missed your show. I am so sorry. What time is it?"

"Don't worry about it. I would take a night off if I could, too." He smiled, pushing my hair from my face.

"I called him."

His smile faded and worry took over.

"I thought you might have. I wish you would have let me be with you."

"I needed to do this on my own. Tucker. I can handle it."

His finger traced the puffy skin under my eye.

"Clearly."

"I'm fine. I promise. You don't need to worry. He wants to see me."

The muscles in Tucker's jaw began to tick under his skin and I knew he wasn't fond of the idea.

"I don't think that's a good idea."

"He has a family." That seemed to shock Tucker because his eyes widened before his nostrils flared. "It's okay. I'm happy for him. I have a family now, too." I was grinning from ear to ear, loving the sound of it.

"You always have, Cass. You have me; you have all of us. You never had to be alone." His thumb slid back and forth over my cheekbone.

"I know that, Tucker. But I owe it to him and to me to get to know him again."

"I'd like to come with you when you do go to see him."

I nodded and he pulled my face closer, placing a kiss on my forehead before pulling my entire body closer to cuddle me. I loved lying in his arms. I felt safe, and no matter what thoughts raced in my head, my heart was full.

I placed my palm on Tucker's chest, feeling his strong, steady heartbeat under my fingertips as I drifted back off into a dreamless sleep.

The next morning I awoke before the guys as usual and slipped out of bed to make some coffee and work on a new song to help get out some of the feelings. I yawned, my eyes connecting with Donna who was sitting at the table reading over a newspaper.

She looked back down at what she was reading as if she hadn't even noticed me. I needed to try to make things right between us and let her know that I had nothing but good intentions. I wanted this band together more than anyone and worked hard to keep it that way. Maybe if she saw where I was coming from, she would let up a little bit with her attitude. It was making life on the bus miserable for everyone.

I reluctantly made my way to the small kitchen area and began to prepare a pot of coffee.

"Would you like a cup?" I asked, turning to look at her. She held up her expensive frothy drink, not bothering to glance in my direction. I rolled my eyes as I turned back to the counter. I suddenly felt like I was back in the diner with a bitchy customer who thought she was too good to acknowledge my existence. It was becoming increasingly hard to not give her a piece of my mind.

"Thank you anyway," she said, and just like that, the tension fizzled out of me and I took a deep calming breath. I poured my coffee and dropped in a few ice cubes. I took a seat directly across from her. She glanced up at me, waiting for me to say something.

"I think we got off on the wrong foot," I began, but she held up her hand to stop me.

"This isn't personal, Cass. I can tell you are probably a good person and you and Tucker are caught up in this . . .

puppy love. I think that is wonderful. Truly. But this is a business, and your relationship is not good for business. Tucker won't be focused and the fans will turn against him and you. If you loved him, you would be on the first flight back to whatever trailer park he picked you up at."

I knew my mouth was hanging open just waiting to catch flies, but I couldn't even begin to form a response that didn't involve me kicking this woman's ass. She smiled and that just made it worse. I glanced down at my cup and for a brief second entertained the idea of giving her a French roast shower. Her gaze followed mine, and her eyes narrowed.

"This isn't just me, Cass. The band and I have discussed it." She lowered her voice as she leaned in closer. "Everyone knows you shouldn't be here, even Tucker. Unfortunately, he cares about you enough that he doesn't want to hurt your feelings. It's sweet, really."

I was certain my heart stopped beating. It clenched painfully in my chest, and the air was knocked out of my lungs.

"I'm going to run some errands. This was a good talk." She winked and slid out of her seat. She slipped off of the bus, leaving me alone to self-destruct. I glanced down at the paper that she had left behind. It was a large picture of the guys from last night's show. Tucker had a girl on each side with his arms draped around their shoulders, a big smile on his face. I knew in my heart it was probably just fans wanting a photo op, but Donna's words kept replaying on a loop in my head.

I didn't know if I was strong enough to handle this anymore.

I didn't know how long I sat there, staring off at the picture before I crumpled it up and shoved it in the small trash can under the kitchen sink. I was leaning over the counter with my eyes closed when a hand fell on my hip.

"Good morning," Tucker said as he kissed my cheek and walked around me to grab a coffee cup. "How'd you sleep?" He poured the dark, rich liquid into the mug.

"Fine." I turned to face him and gave him a smile. He narrowed his eyes as he took a sip of his drink. "You sure you're okay?"

"Yeah. I'm fine. Just thinking of that call with my dad."

He smiled as he took a step closer and put a hand on my shoulder.

"Everything is going to be fine."

I nodded but didn't know what else to say. Suddenly everything felt different. Once again I found myself doubting where I fit into his life.

"I know I was kind of a dick about it, but I think you should go see him. You were right. He's your dad. He deserves a second chance."

That didn't help. Was he trying to get rid of me? I felt like I was ready to vomit.

"Yeah. I think that would be good."

"Pills," Eric yelled from his bunk, and Tucker laughed,

shaking his head. I was happy to put an end to the painfully awkward conversation. I dug through the cupboard and grabbed Eric's medication and a bottle of water from the tiny fridge.

I walked back to his bunk and stuck my hand just inside the curtain.

"Jesus Christ," Eric squealed as the ice-cold bottle came in contact with his bare chest.

"Sorry!" It was just one of those days.

I slipped into the bathroom and pulled the door closed, leaning over the sink and slowly raising my eyes to look at myself in the mirror. I wasn't that weak little girl from the trailer park. I could get past this. But my heart still felt like it had been crushed by Donna's words, and seeing that picture of Tucker caused it to crumble. I wanted to run away. I needed to escape everything that was hurting me deep inside and figure out who I was and what I wanted in life. I needed to see my father. The escape would give me a much-needed break from the tour and get to know my father again. How could I ever really know myself without knowing where I came from? I turned on the sink and splashed water on my face, grimacing at the heavy bags under my eyes. At least they weren't bruises. I had come a long way and needed to remember that.

A light tapping at the door pulled me from my pity party. I slid it open to see Tucker leaning against the wall and grinning.

"Want some company?" He winked and my heart melted.

"I was thinking about some breakfast." I walked around him, grinning.

"Fine. We can do dessert later."

I grabbed some fresh clothes from the cabinets beside our bunks. I barely had any space for my belongings now that Donna had taken over the large room at the back of the bus.

"What's wrong?" Tucker asked as he grabbed clothes from his compartment. I realized I had been scowling as I thought of her.

"Nothing. Just not sure what to wear."

"Sarah really is rubbing off on you." He laughed and I threw a shirt at him and he ducked out of the way. I grabbed a pair of jeans and a purple tank top and stood just as Donna entered the bus. She froze, watching me.

"Leaving?" she asked with a raised eyebrow. I narrowed my eyes at her.

"Going out for breakfast. Want to come?" Tucker was completely oblivious to the tension between us.

"No." She sank down onto the kitchen table bench as she looked around. "What happened to my paper?"

Tucker and I walked between the bunks toward the front door.

"We're running low on toilet paper. I would check the bathroom," I said.

Eric chuckled loudly from his bunk and I smirked, making sure to look her in the eye as I passed.

ತಮರರರ

"You guys all right?" Tucker asked as we stepped out into the parking lot. "I know she isn't exactly warm to the idea of you being here."

I put my arms around his neck and stared into his deep-blue eyes.

"Everything is perfect as long as I'm with you." I gave him a chaste kiss on the lips before pulling him across the lot to a Denny's that sat on the other side of the highway.

I never got to finish my coffee and was in desperate need to fill up on caffeine. I wasn't going to think about any of the drama until I was properly awake and thinking more clearly. Rash decisions had hurt those I loved in the past, and I wouldn't make those mistakes again. Tucker didn't deserve to be the victim of my fears; I owed it to him to work it out.

"I want something sugary."

I laughed, looking up at the man I had fallen so hard for. It was hard to sit in this diner and not remember the first day he showed up in my diner. It felt like a lifetime ago and so much had changed, but I still got butterflies in my stomach when he smiled at me.

"I like this."

He pulled his eyebrows together, not sure of what I meant.

"I like spending time with you alone without all the outside . . ."

"Bullshit?" He smiled, and I couldn't help but laugh.

"Yes. I like it when we are alone," I replied honestly.

"I like our alone time, too." He raised his eyebrow.

"I'm serious. I miss this. Sneaking off to be by ourselves . . . it's nice."

"Why don't we plan an escape? Get a hotel room or something."

"I'd love that."

"Can I get you something to drink?" the waitress asked, and I blushed, not realizing she had been standing at the edge of our table.

"Orange juice for me, please."

"Chocolate milk." Tucker gave her his jaw-dropping grin, and my mind flashed to the image from the newspaper. I shook the thought from my mind and plastered a smile on my face. I needed to trust him. I couldn't let Donna get inside of my head. But it wasn't Donna. The picture was there in black and white. That was it. The seed had been planted in a moment of weakness, and now it was festering, sprouting into a full-blown meltdown.

"I'll also take a coffee, black," I said with my eyes watching Tucker. His eyebrows scrunched together as he stared at me. The waitress went to grab our drinks.

"How is the writing going?"

"It's going." I could feel myself closing off, and I felt powerless to fight against it.

CHAPTER

Fourteen

IT HAD BEEN two weeks since I had made contact with my father, and I had called him four times since our initial conversation. Tucker was apprehensive about me letting him back in my life, but I began to make plans to take a trip to New Orleans for a visit. The band would be busy with new interviews that Donna had lined up, starting with a television interview on the local news channel in Ellisburg. As cruel as she behaved toward me, even I could see how good she had been for the band in the short time she had been with them. Today was proof of that.

I was incredibly excited to see Tucker on television. It wasn't the first time, but when I had seen him before, it was while we were separated. Back then it had broken my heart seeing him and knowing he was so far away.

"We should go out for drinks. Have girl's time after this."

Sarah propped herself up on her elbows as we kept our eyes glued to the small flat-screen in the front of the bus.

I nodded as the show began and the butterflies in my belly took flight. The newscaster was talking about Damaged and showing pictures of the band. I squealed when the camera panned out and the guys sat on a couch next to her.

"They look so good!" I clutched my heart necklace that dangled from my neck. She began her interview asking about tour dates and how they liked life on the road, how well they all got along and all of the other mundane questions that were standard in these interviews.

"We're like brothers. We fight from time to time, but five minutes later it's like it never happened." Tucker took a sip from a glass of water that sat on the small table in front of him.

"Rumor has it you boys will be playing at the Video Music Awards in a few weeks. What have you been doing to prepare for a show like that?" the woman asked.

"We have been rehearsing, just like we do for all of our shows. But the stakes are higher for this gig, for sure. Definitely more nerve-racking." Tucker grinned, and the girls in the audience went crazy.

"I'm sure it's like riding a bike for you by now. Your touring schedule has been hectic. That must make it difficult to maintain any sense of normalcy . . . or relations outside of the band."

Tucker's eyes darted off to the left, and I knew he was looking for Donna. He shifted in his seat, clearing his throat before picking up his water and taking another sip.

"Of course it makes it harder, but like any relationship, if you want it to work, you have to be willing to make the time for it." His eyes went to the camera, and I felt like he was staring directly at me. He had just admitted, sort of, that he was with someone, and my heart began to flutter as I raised up on my knees and clutched my arms around myself. It would be major for him to proclaim his love for me to the world, and I didn't realize how important that was to me until this moment. Most celebrities tried to keep those details private, but after my ambush interview, the cat was let out of the bag. Tucker was told not to confirm or deny his involvement with me, to keep his female admirers happy. I understood, but it definitely hurt.

"Like many singers, most of your songs come from life experiences. What can you tell me about 'Empty Sheets'?"

Tucker paused and waited for the fans in the audience to quiet down before answering.

"It's obviously about someone who had gone through a very tough relationship, and I think a lot of people can really relate to it. Everyone has been hurt or felt alone at some point in their lives," he answered.

"It is heartbreakingly beautiful. You're a very gifted songwriter."

"Thank you." Tucker ran his hand from the back of his hair to the front.

"Did he just . . ." Sarah sat up and pointed to the television.

"I don't know." I grabbed the remote and turned off the television as the interview ended, in shock that Tucker seemed to be taking credit for my words. My intensely personal words. This was the only thing in the world that was mine, that I could lay claim to and take some pride in, and just like that it was taken from me.

"I'm sure he was told to say that."

"It doesn't matter. He shouldn't have." I pushed to my feet and began pacing the floor as I chewed angrily on my lower lip. "I think I'll take you up on that drink now."

I didn't waste any time getting off that bus. I felt like I was drowning inside of that closed-off space that not long ago I actually considered home.

"It's Donna. She is slowly trying to put herself in the middle of my relationship," I said as we went inside the bar.

"She can't come between the two of you unless you let her."

"Trust me. I am not." I slid onto the bar stool and Sarah took a seat next to me, holding up a hand to signal the bartender.

"Maybe not you . . ." Her voice trailed off.

"She's been pulling us apart from day one, but this is different. Those songs are my heart and soul. It is the only thing I have of my own."

"Two shots of Jack," she told the bartender who flipped his cleaning rag over his shoulder and went to work at pouring our drinks. "I want to hire you." She turned to face me.

"Hire me for what?" I drank back my whiskey, wincing as it burned my throat.

"You're an amazing writer, and we could use some fresh material."

"I don't think that's a good idea." I felt like selling my songs to someone else would be like cheating on Tucker. As much as he had hurt me, I didn't want to go behind his back.

"You don't want to follow your dreams and see where they take you?"

"I don't know what I want anymore. I never really had a dream outside of escaping my old life. I didn't know I was good at anything."

"You have talent, that's for sure. But is it what you want out of life?"

"I enjoy writing and it helps me work through all of my issues. It would be incredible to be able to do that for a living."

"Then you need to make it happen. You can't rely on anyone but yourself to do that. Not even Tucker, no matter how close you are."

After a few more drinks Sarah had to get ready for the concert tonight. I didn't feel like watching the band perform. I was always a few feet from Tucker, but it might as well have been thousands of miles. When he was onstage he was a product, an object that belonged to the masses. It didn't used to feel that way, but ever since Donna had taken over as manager, things had changed. I bit my tongue because I knew that was what was best for the band, but what I wanted was what was best for Tucker. I wasn't sure what that was anymore.

"I'm gonna take a walk, clear my head."

"Don't get lost. Concert starts at eight," Sarah replied.

I nodded, not wanting to tell her I didn't think I could handle watching Tucker perform tonight. I needed a break. I watched Sarah leave and waited a few minutes before stepping outside and figuring out where I was going to go from here.

I decided to go see a movie instead. It was such a normal mundane thing, but it was a luxury for me. I hadn't been able to afford things like that most of my life, and now I just didn't have the time, even though I felt like ninety percent of my day was spent sitting and waiting.

I headed for the large theater across the highway and purchased a ticket for *Halftime*, a new comedy that I had heard nothing about since we rarely watched television. It didn't matter. I just needed to do something fun on my own for once. I couldn't let my happiness be determined by others any longer.

The film dragged on, and I spent more time watching a group of college friends laugh and make fun of each other than I did watching the movie.

After the last of the credits rolled up the screen and the lights to the theater came back on, I decided I had been gone long enough.

My mood had lightened a little and it felt good to collect

my thoughts instead of going with my normal instinct to flee. Even with all that was going on, it gave me hope that I was finally growing as a person. In my mind I began laying out a calm, levelheaded way to approach Tucker.

All feelings of contentment left as I approached the bus. I could see Tucker pacing back and forth in front of the door. When he spotted me he began to walk toward me and it was obvious he was not happy.

"I have been searching everywhere for you. I was worried sick. I thought . . ." Tucker cut off his own thoughts as the muscles in his jaw ticked under his skin.

"It's a little too late to be worried about me," I spat back angrily, my hands on my hips. So much for keeping a level head and talking this out like adults.

"I missed a concert! Do you have any idea how pissed everyone is at me right now?"

I took a step forward, staring him dead in the eye.

"Do you have any idea how pissed *I* am at you right now?" I spat.

"You're mad at *me*?" He had the nerve to look offended, and I wanted to scream. He really had no clue how badly he had hurt me. "This is my career, Cass. You told me not to give up on it, and now you're doing your best to destroy it."

I took a step back. It felt like I had been physically punched in the gut. His words ripped through me. I was Tucker's biggest supporter.

"What about me, Tucker? What about *my* dreams?" I had finally found something I was good at and I loved to do, and it got swept under the giant rug that was Tucker's fame. I couldn't handle it anymore. I needed to have my own identity.

"I have no idea what you are talking about."

"Writing that poem . . . that *song* . . . was the one thing I had done for me since I joined you on tour. It was mine. I had created something I was incredibly proud of, and you took credit for it like it meant nothing at all." I knew I was overreacting, but I felt like I was slipping away. I couldn't stand in the shadows of his career anymore. I was getting lost in the dark.

"Cass, our fans don't want to know that I have a girlfriend. They don't want to know that I am singing songs that I didn't write myself."

"Well, someone has been spending too much time with Donna." I crossed my arms over my chest.

"Don't do that. You know that this band is important to me."

"I used to be important to you, too. What happened to that?" I asked as I took off around him, walking as fast as I could to the bus door. I yanked it open, unable to look at him as the tears threatened to spill over. I felt like a jerk. I didn't want him to agonize over choosing between me and his band. I wanted the choice to be obvious. I wanted him to stand up for me. I didn't want to be his dirty little secret.

CHAPTER

Fifteen

I SLEPT LIKE HELL all night tossing and turning. Tucker never came to bed, and I knew everyone was mad at him and blamed me for it. This tour—our rhythm, our lack of privacy, this whole situation—it was killing us, and we needed a drastic change or it would destroy our relationship for good.

It didn't take long to decide it was time to visit my father. It would give Tucker and me the breathing room we needed to think about what we wanted out of life and what we needed from each other.

I grabbed my cell phone and sent him a text. *I want to visit my father.*

I waited for nearly ten minutes for his response, and it was killing me not knowing where he was. *I found a flight that leaves tomorrow.*

I didn't know what I wanted him to say, but that wasn't it.

He was happy to send me away and he wasn't going to put up a fight. As tears swam in my eyes, I grabbed my small duffel bag and began to shove some clothes inside.

"Trying to sleep," Eric called from his bunk.

"Sorry," I said sadly, my voice cracking.

He pushed back the curtain to his bunk and groaned as he sat up.

"Where the hell are you going?" he asked, pointing to my bag.

"To see my father."

"You coming back?"

I stopped shoving clothes in my bag and took a deep breath.

"I don't think I'm wanted around here anymore."

Eric jumped down from the bunk and put his hand on my shoulder, turning me around to face him.

"You don't honestly believe that, do you?"

I couldn't respond. The words stuck behind the lump that had formed in my throat. Eric looked uncomfortable as he scratched the back of his head.

"Tucker would quit this band in a heartbeat if you asked him to."

"I wouldn't do that," I said defensively.

"I know you wouldn't. You care too much about him to ask him something like that. This isn't easy for you; we all know that. It only proves how much you both love each other.

You think he would throw it all away over some bullshit fight?"

I shook my head. For once, Eric was the voice of reason.

"He fell asleep on Filth's bus. They have a free bunk. He just needed some time to think. I told him it was stupid, but he was sure you didn't want him here."

"It's his bus."

"But you're his girl, and that is more important to him than all of this."

"Thank you . . . for saying that." I was grateful for his kindness, but I wished I believed his words.

"It's what friends do. Now stop your blubbering."

I laughed and sank back on the bed feeling the pressure leave my chest.

THE BAND was out the door early to rehearse and discuss the music video they would be shooting next week.

Tucker came back around six in the evening and barely spoke a word to me, but I could see he wasn't mad. He was concerned about me leaving. Tucker had reservations from the beginning about me reconnecting with my father. He didn't trust a man who would leave behind everyone he was supposed to love.

"What time is my flight?" I asked as I picked up my sub sandwich and took a bite.

"Nine in the morning." He took a sip of his soda but didn't look up at me.

"Three days?"

He nodded as he shoved a handful of chips in his mouth.

"Can you please talk to me? We can't work through this if we don't talk. I hate you being mad at me."

"I'm not mad at you, Cass." His eyes met mine. "I'm scared you are going to get hurt or taken advantage of by one of the few people who you love. Not that he deserves it." The muscles in his jaw ticked.

"People change. Look at me. I'm a completely different person now."

"No, you're not, Cass. You are the same sweet and loving girl I fell in love with. Your circumstances changed, not who you are."

"You don't think he is any different?"

"I hope he is, for your sake."

We spent the rest of the evening in Tucker's bunk, wrapped in each other's arms as we stared up at the pictures taped overhead. There was still so much that needed to be said, but we were both exhausted, physically and emotionally.

"What's that one from?" I asked, pointing to a picture of him surrounded by a bunch of children ranging in age from toddlers to late teens.

"That's when we played a free gig for the West Lake Children's Home. All of those kids were abused, abandoned, or neglected. Every single one of them had a smile on their faces that day. We raised a few thousand dollars for them."

"That's amazing. I would have loved to have been there."

He pulled me tighter into his arms and kissed the side of my head.

"You will be at the next one."

I twisted to look up at him, his head above mine.

"I promised we'd do it every year. Remind us who we are and how fortunate we are to be doing this."

"You really are lucky."

His gaze fell to my lips and back to my eyes as he ran his thumb over my chin.

"I'm the luckiest man on Earth." He tilted my chin up higher to meet his lips. "I'm going to miss you."

I laid my head on his shoulder, my arm over his chest. We drifted off to sleep in each other's arms.

I FELT LIKE I was on another planet leaving Tucker and the band behind to go meet my father. I wished I had Tucker by my side for this, but it was something I needed to do for myself. Tucker couldn't hold my hand for the rest of my life and he had a very hectic schedule to maintain.

New Orleans was unlike anything I had ever seen. We had some crazy characters on the River Walk in Savannah, but they didn't hold a candle to the street performers that lined the city here. Everything was painted in bright colors and it looked like the city was in the midst of a party, even though it wasn't anywhere near a holiday. My eyes danced over the buildings. I promised Eric I would take a picture of the House of the Rising Sun if I saw it, but the cabdriver had no idea what I was talking about.

The driver took me right through the French Quarter at my request. I was eager to see my dad but was so terrified that it would go badly that I was trying to prolong the inevitable as much as possible.

The car crawled at a snail's pace as we got stuck behind a horse carriage, and tourists stood in the streets to take pictures of the beautiful old balconies covered in bead necklaces.

I glanced down at my cell phone, wanting to call Tucker, but, even after our tender night together, all of the tension between us in the last few weeks made me worry he might be relieved to have a break from me. I wouldn't blame him. I was sad to admit that getting out of that cramped bus actually felt good. I missed Tucker desperately, though, and that was even more reason to give us some time apart. I didn't want to rely on him for my happiness or to feel fulfilled. I needed to get that on my own.

As we pulled back out onto the main road I began to think about the other man I was missing in my life, my father. The trip from the quarter to his home was only about five minutes, but it flew by so quickly I wanted to yell at the driver to slow down. My stomach was in knots.

We pulled up to the curb in front of a modest home that was painted a pale yellow with purple trim around the windows. It sat several feet off the ground on large cinder blocks. I got out of the back of the car and paid the cabdriver, clutching my bag to my side. I felt a million miles from home, even though I had no home to speak of.

The screen door opened and an older man stepped out into the sun. I recognized him instantly—he looked exactly as he had when I was young, but his hair was much thinner and his midsection had expanded.

"Welcome home, Cass." He had a huge smile on his face, and my heart warmed at his words. He held his arms open, and I reluctantly stepped up the front steps and gave him a quick hug. The door opened behind us and out stepped a woman with an enormous round belly. Her hand rested on top of it, and the other hand rested on her lower back.

"Nice to see you, Cass," she said as if I was just stopping by and had done it a million times before. It was comforting. I held out my hand to shake hers, but she waved it away and pulled me in for a hug. She had deep-brown hair cut off in a bob at her chin and a warm smile.

"I'm June, of course, but you can call me just about anything you like. You're such a pretty little thing. You didn't tell me she was so darn pretty!" She looked back at my father who laughed.

"I did too tell her you was pretty. Don't let her say otherwise."

"Oh, you know that's not what I meant. Don't you go making this girl think we talk bad." She scolded him, and I laughed, watching their easy, carefree interaction. "Come on in and see your brother. He won't stop going on and on about you."

She opened the door and I stepped inside, my eyes scanning the small space. The house smelled of mildew, and the paint was peeling off the walls. It looked yellow, but I think it was just the age. The furniture was a hodgepodge of yard-sale finds and things taken from the trash. A large sign hung on the wall that read *Laissez le bon temps rouler*. My father's eyes followed mine and he smiled.

"Let the good times roll." He patted me on the shoulder. It was fitting. I knew we had more than our share of things to discuss, but for now it felt good just to be in his presence. I wanted to be mad, to scream at him, but it was hard to be mad at someone who had escaped his shitty life to find happiness. That is exactly what I had done. He couldn't have known how things had gone downhill with Mom.

"Ryley!" June yelled much louder than necessary for the small dwelling. A little boy came out from one of the bedrooms at the back of the house. He had thick deep-brown hair like his mother and blue eyes that matched my father's and mine. June had green eyes, and I was happy that Ryley seemed to have something from our side of the family. "Come say hi to your sister."

He was shy, looking down at a large Lego toy in his hands. I sank down on my knees to get to his eye level.

"Hello, Ryley. My name is Cass." I didn't feel comfortable telling him I was his sister. It felt a little strange to just fling myself into their family.

"Hi," he said quietly, still pretending to ignore me, but he glanced up at me to look at my face when he thought I wasn't looking.

"That looks like a fun toy."

"Daddy got it for me." It shouldn't sting to hear him call my father his own, but it did and I knew I wouldn't be able to brush the past under the rug. We would have to sit down and work out what had happened in order to move on. I tousled Ryley's hair, and he ran off to disappear back into the room he had been hiding in.

"He's a little shy," June explained, and she made her way into the kitchen and pulled open the fridge. "Sweet tea?"

"Sure. That would be great."

My father motioned toward the table and I nodded, sitting down at the little table. He took a seat across from me in a mismatched chair.

"Donated," he explained when he saw me looking it over. "We lost our things in Katrina and had to move here."

"You lost everything?"

He smiled as June sat down a glass in front of each of us. He put his hand on her stomach and placed a kiss in the center.

"Not everything. We had each other. That was all we needed."

It was incredibly moving to hear him speak that way. As a child I rarely remember him saying anything that wasn't derogatory to my mom.

"You seem very happy together." I took a sip of the tea and gave June a smile. "Thank you."

"It's been a struggle. That's for sure."

"Did you get help? Didn't the government send help?"

"They did, princess, but there was so many of us needing help. There was only so much they could do. We got us one of those trailers, but the smell from the material they built it with made June so sick she could hardly get out of bed. We were forced to find somewhere else to go. I lost my job over at the plant. It went underwater, and so I have been helping people get back on their feet and doing odd jobs for local businesses, but as everything got back to normal the work fell off."

"That's awful." I looked at June's growing belly and thought of my brother in the other room. How were they going to survive? I admired their cautiously optimistic outlook in light of all they were facing. They could have blamed the world, but they stuck together and were happy to have each other. My phone rang and I smiled as Tucker's name scrolled across the screen.

"Do you mind?" I didn't want to interrupt as we were finally talking, but I knew Tucker wouldn't have a lot of free time.

"You take your time, sweetie," June said with a grin.

I made my way out onto the small front porch and answered the call.

"How was the flight?" I didn't realize how much I had missed his voice.

"It was great. Really great."

"How was meeting your dad?"

"Better than I expected. He's nicer than I remember, and June is really, really sweet. I feel so bad for them."

"Why would you feel bad for them?"

"They lost everything in that hurricane and are struggling hard to make ends meet."

He sighed heavily into the phone and didn't respond.

"What? What's wrong?"

"Did they ask you for money, sweetheart?"

"No. Of course not." I didn't know why I acted like I was offended. I barely knew these people, family or not, and was a little too eager to take up their defense.

"Please tell me if he does. I don't want him taking advantage of you."

"Geez, Tucker. Can you take a break from trying to save the day just once? If you're so worried about me getting hurt, why don't you tell Donna to fuck off?" I closed my eyes, waiting for the backlash to my comment. I shouldn't have opened my big mouth. Tucker didn't need me coming between him and the band, and Donna was now part of that group. I was the outsider. "I'm sorry. I shouldn't have said that. I am just really tired and overwhelmed."

"No. You're right. What do you want me to do, Cass, because I'm getting mixed signals. One minute you're telling me to stay with the band and the next you're fighting with me about it. I don't know what it is you want me to do."

"Nothing. I don't want you to do anything. Donna and I will work out whatever our problem is. . . . I'm sorry I brought it up."

"I know she is a bitch to you. I have talked to her about that. Believe me, there is nothing more that I want than for you two to get along. There needs to be some compromise on both sides."

I wanted to scream. I didn't do anything to Donna, and she was making it a point to make our lives miserable, but for once I bit my tongue and agreed with him. There was no use in stressing him out before a show.

June stepped out onto the porch and smiled at me, and I grinned back politely.

"I should go. I'll call you later."

"You better. I love you."

"I love you, too," I replied and ended the call, looking up at June.

"I didn't mean to interrupt. I was just going for my evening walk. They say it helps move things along with the baby. Would you like to join me? Your daddy is putting Ryley down for the night."

"Sure." I followed her down the uneven steps of the front porch, and we began to walk down the sidewalk.

The air was muggy and I wished I hadn't worn jeans because they felt like they were sticking to my skin. Anyone who said Georgia heat is comparable to Louisiana had obviously never lived in this place.

"When are you due?" I asked as we continued our slow pace down the old sidewalk.

"I have three more weeks." She smiled, rubbing over her belly. "Ryley came two weeks late."

"Yikes." We both laughed, and some of the tension eased between us. It was odd talking to the woman my father was in love with and not knowing the first thing about her. "Are you from here?"

"Born in raised in Baton Rouge. Moved here about a year before I met your daddy."

"What can you tell me about him? I don't remember much from when I was little."

"He loves his football and grilling in the summer. He has the biggest heart."

"He seems so . . . different." I wasn't sure if that would be taken as an insult, but it felt like it had to be said.

"How so?"

"I don't know. I remember him and my momma fighting a lot when I was little, over money, mostly." I shrugged and turned the corner to round the block.

"Well, that can be pretty stressful."

I felt like I had touched on a sore subject, but it made me wonder if things weren't as perfect as they seemed.

"Do you work?" I asked, staring off at a group of people ahead. Someone was playing a saxophone and others were gathered around singing.

"I used to sing at the local joints." She beamed as she shook her head. "I was something to see. Before this big old belly, I could really draw a crowd. That's how I met your father."

"You quit when you got pregnant?"

"Not long after we had gotten together things went all pear shaped." She glanced down at her stomach. "Wasn't many wanting to see a big old pregnant woman up onstage, and your daddy . . ." Her voice trailed off, and I could tell the thought had made her sad so I didn't press her. I remembered all too well how my father wanted my mother to stop pursuing her dreams as a hairstylist so she could stay home and keep an eye on me.

We had made a loop around the block and were coming back up on the tiny yellow house.

"I'm really glad you came, Cass. It is truly great to have the whole family together."

"Thanks. I was really glad he called me. I mean, definitely a surprise since it has been so long . . . but a good one."

She made a face but soon covered it with another bright smile and we made our way up the steps to the front door.

My father stepped outside before we could enter.

"Shhh . . . That boy was fighting sleep something fierce."

"I'm gonna run in and use the ladies' room." June stood on her tiptoes and kissed my father on the cheek before slipping inside. He motioned to the steps and sat down on the top one. I took a seat next to him and watched as the sun began to sink behind the buildings.

"You have a nice family," I said, staring off into the distance.

"Thank you. You know you are welcome here any time."

I nodded, but it didn't feel that way. I felt like an outsider.

"June is really sweet. I like her."

"She's a spitfire." He chuckled. "Tell me about this boy you're seeing."

"He's a really great guy. He has an amazing voice."

"Makes good money at that I'm sure."

I nodded. I wanted to stay off the topic of money. I didn't want Tucker to be right.

"We don't talk about that sort of thing." I shrugged as I ran my hands over my jeans. "How do you deal with this humidity?"

"You'd be surprised what your body can get used to." He chuckled. I thought back on the bruises that used to mar my body and nodded in agreement. It was incredibly awkward trying to carry on a conversation with him alone, and I wished

June would hurry up, but I was sure she was leaving us be on purpose.

"What a . . ." He cleared his throat. "What happened to your momma?"

My chest tightened.

I explained my turbulent relationship with Jax and how we struggled every day to make it. I hated to tell him about my mother's drug use, but I felt he should know the desperation she felt. When I told him about my relationship with Tucker and how it had played a major part in the way the events unfolded, I braced myself for his judgment, but he only nodded and listened.

"I didn't know how bad it had gotten for you," he said, and his eyes met mine.

June stepped out onto the porch behind us, and I was thankful to be pulled back from our trip down memory lane.

"Am I interrupting?" she asked as she looked between my father and me.

"Not at all," I replied, clearing my throat.

"I grabbed some beignets from Café Du Monde today. Thought you'd like one."

"That would be great. What is it?" I looked to my father and he chuckled.

"Fancy donut with lots of sugar on it."

June went back in the house and returned a few seconds later with a bag full of food. I grabbed one and took a bite as we ate in silence, watching the sunset behind the buildings.

"They are delicious. Thank you."

June smiled, proud to share a little piece of her home with me.

"Expensive," my father mumbled.

"You guys didn't need to spend money on me." I felt guilty after all of their talk of losing everything that I hadn't even thought twice about her buying treats especially for me. I pushed the thought of my father being the cause of my suffering as a child to the back of my mind.

"It's no worry. You're family." June waved her hand in the air. "You must be exhausted from all that flying. I'll go make up the couch for you."

"That's great. Thank you." My father and I sat in silence for a few minutes. I wanted to bring up the fact that he left, what it did to my momma and me, but I couldn't get up the nerve. He had invited me into his home and it felt wrong. I could feel his eyes on me, and I wanted to break the awkward silence.

"I started writing. Songs mostly. Well, it's poetry really, but Tucker has sung one at his concert." I was rambling. I didn't understand this sudden nervousness and need for his approval.

He nodded but didn't say anything. I was surprised when it stung to have this man, a stranger by all accounts, not acknowledge what I felt was a big achievement.

"I should get some sleep." I pushed to my feet and dusted the dirt from the back of my legs.

"See you in the morning."

"Good night."

That night I dreamed that I was back on the bus. I missed snuggling up next to Tucker. It didn't matter what state we were in or where we were headed, I was always home in his arms and I missed that. I wasn't sure what I thought I would find down in Louisiana, but this wasn't it. I had hoped that my father's life had turned around and he was happy, but the house was in shambles and they seemed to worry constantly about where their next dollar would come from. Instead of feeling like I'd found my way home, I felt like a guest, a stranger in this foreign city, this unfamiliar house. And worse, I felt sad for my father. I felt pity for him and wished there was something I could do to help him and June in the wake of the tragedy they'd suffered.

The next morning I woke to Ryley pushing his finger against my eye. I rolled over and tickled his stomach, causing him to giggle and run away.

"You leave her alone, young man." June was in the kitchen cooking something on the stove. It smelled like sausage, and my stomach growled. "Breakfast will be ready in a few minutes. Eggs and boudin."

"Sounds . . . good." I didn't know what it was, but it smelled incredible.

"Keep it down, June," my father yelled from his bedroom, startling me. June made a face at me, and I laughed quietly to myself. I walked into the kitchen to see if she needed any help.

"Anything I can do?"

"You can grab the plates." With her spatula, she pointed to the cabinet next to the fridge. I set the table, not sure if my father would be joining us for breakfast or not. I figured it was better safe than sorry, so I set the table for four.

He eventually rolled out of bed as June finished up. He gave her a kiss on the cheek as he stole a piece of sausage, and she smacked him on the hand.

We didn't talk about my mother and what had happened after he left. I realized it was more important to me to get a fresh start, not rehash the past. I wanted to spend some time with them just getting to know them better. We would have plenty of opportunities down the road to revisit the heavy baggage of our past.

CHAPTER

Sixteen

I RAN INTO TUCKER'S arms, and he lifted me from the ground, spinning us.

"I have missed you so much," he said as he sat me back on the ground and placed a hand on either side of my face. "How was your trip?"

"It was good. A little strange . . . but I'm glad I went."

"Come on. We have a long ride ahead of us, and I can't be late for the shoot."

"You started shooting the music video? I thought that wasn't until next week."

"Change of plans."

"I could have taken a cab, Tucker. You didn't need to pick me up from the airport."

"I wanted to see you as soon as possible." He kissed me on the forehead, and I breathed in his scent of coconut.

We made our way out to his bike, and I slid on the back, wrapping my arms around his waist. I could ride with him all day long. I loved being so close to him and feeling like we were in our own little world.

After a few hours we pulled into the studio parking lot. My legs felt like jelly as I slid off the bike and stretched. Tucker did the same, looking pained from the round-trip he had made.

"You really didn't need to come get me."

"I really did." He smiled and placed a kiss on my forehead. He looped his fingers in mine as we began to walk to the giant glass doors.

"I'm surprised Donna let you leave."

"She doesn't control me, Cass." The anger in his voice made my heart rate accelerate. I hadn't meant to insult him.

"That's not what I meant. I'm sorry."

He nodded and pulled open the door, waiting for me to walk through. I released his hand and stepped inside as he placed his hand on the small of my back and followed me.

The lobby was large but rustic. Everything was concrete, and brown swirling paintings hung all around the receptionist's desk. It felt very masculine and cavelike, but done in an upscale manor.

"Welcome back, Mr. White."

Tucker smiled at the woman sitting behind the counter who had a severe black bob. Her lips quirked into a smile as she picked up a phone and spoke quietly into the receiver.

We walked to the back of the room where there was a large set of medieval double doors made of a deep gray metal, lined in rivets. Tucker pulled it open, once again waiting for me to step inside before he followed. We followed the hall to the third door on the left with a bright red light over the door, signaling someone was working inside.

I was shocked as he pulled the door open. The room was massive with a giant green screen plastered across the back wall and a motorcycle, much like Tucker's, in front of it. To the right was another screen and all of the band's equipment. Eric was playing the drums as a man guided him on which direction to look. To the left was an elegant room that looked like the bedroom out of a mansion, complete with white silk sheets and a pile of pillows. That threw me for a loop, and I stopped walking, causing Tucker to run into my back. He gripped my hips and guided me forward as Donna's eyes found us. She narrowed them, and I swallowed back the anger I instantaneously felt when she was around. I had a long couple of days trying to get reacquainted with my father, and I was in no mood to put up with Donna's shit. She stalked toward us, folding her arms across her chest.

"I expected you an hour ago." Her eyes were glued on Tucker.

"My flight ran late," I chimed in. Her gaze flicked to me and back to Tucker.

"We are almost ready for you. Makeup is waiting." She walked away with a loud huff.

"Makeup?" I laughed and spun around to face Tucker. He grinned and shook his head.

"I didn't like the idea either." He laughed and pulled me in to kiss him. I pressed my lips against his, letting my eyes flutter closed.

"Save the passion for the video, Tucker," a man's voice called from behind us, and I pulled back, immediately embarrassed by our public display of affection, but Tucker kept his grip around my waist. Tucker laughed and pulled me against his chest for a hug.

"You sure you want to be here for this?"

I furrowed my brow, searching his eyes.

"I wouldn't miss it for the world." I gave him a smile, but there was a look of concern in his eyes. "Go get ready before the wicked witch casts a spell on me."

He laughed, shaking his head as he made his way to a back corner of the room toward a door that read DRESSING ROOM. I crossed my arms over my stomach as I wandered toward Terry and Chris who were hanging out against the far right wall. They smiled and greeted me when they noticed me, and I felt more at ease in the strange place.

"How's it going?" I asked as I watched a petite blonde blot Terry's cheek with makeup.

"They're making us bitches, Cass," Chris whined, and I snorted as the woman gave him a glare.

Two women walked toward us, and I realized they were

twins as well. They wore only white bikinis and had tattoos covering their bodies. My eyes danced over the artwork on their skin, in awe at how beautiful they were.

"It's not real," one said with a heavy accent that I couldn't place.

"You're kidding?" I stepped closer to inspect the fake tattoos. "That's incredible."

"Thank you," the woman who was still correcting the other twin's makeup called over her shoulder to me.

"Girls," called out the man who had spoken to Tucker earlier. I assumed he was a director or producer or something to that effect, but I didn't want to ask and look stupid. The female twins scurried past me in their towering high heels and made their way to the bed. My stomach tied in knots as I looked back at Chris and Terry.

"It's for our scene," Terry spoke up, alleviating my fears. I sighed and smiled back at him, grateful he put my mind at ease. I glanced back over my shoulder at the man as he had the women sprawl out over the bed, positioning them like human Barbie dolls until he had them at the angle he preferred.

He yelled for Chris and Terry who had large smiles on their faces as they hurried to join the women. I backed against the wall and watched as they climbed into the bed, happier than I had ever seen them. I rolled my eyes and the makeup artist smiled as she watched me.

"First time?" she asked, and I wasn't sure what she meant, but her question sent a blush spreading over my skin like wildfire. "Music video, I mean."

"Yeah." I nodded as I watched the twins begin to make out with their female counterparts as the camera moved closer to them.

"It's not that bad. All make-believe. They look like they are enjoying themselves now, but I guarantee you that when the day is over, they will be exhausted and miserable." I raised my eyebrows as I watched their hands roam all over the women.

"Somehow I doubt that."

She laughed and patted me on the shoulder before disappearing behind the door that Tucker had gone in earlier. My eyes shifted to Eric as he continued to take direction and figure out the best way to shoot his part of the video.

A few minutes passed and four women came out of the makeup area, giggling.

"He is such a good kisser." One of them laughed as the other scoffed.

"Please, his hands were all over my body."

I stiffened, wondering who they were referring to. Eric glanced up and shot them a wink, causing them to erupt in a fit of giggles. I sighed and relaxed back into the wall. I don't know what had gotten into me, but the entire situation was beginning to overwhelm me. I knew Tucker was a rock star and this was what he wanted out of life, but I didn't know how much of the lifestyle he intended to partake in.

After nearly twenty minutes of watching Eric flirt with the girls and the twins rolling around in bed with the other twins, I was beginning to fall asleep. I sank down against the wall and yawned as I watched them shoot scene after scene of what looked like the same thing.

"Tucker," a girl squealed, and I turned to see Tucker come out of the back room. He was wearing a plain white cotton tee and dark-wash jeans. He looked like he always did, and I wondered what they could have been doing to him for so long. The girl was in front of him, partially obstructing my view, but he glanced around her and winked at me, causing my heart to melt in my chest.

I stood, stretching, still sore from the long ride on the back of Tucker's bike. The director called Tucker over to him and began giving him direction. I wanted to walk over, but Donna beat me to it, and I knew, as much as I hated it, this was part of her job and I had no place in it.

Eric made his way to me with a huge grin on his face.

"Twenty bucks says I can fuck at least two of them before the day is over."

I cringed at his crude comment, but it secretly made me happy for him that he was moving past his crush on Sarah.

"Shouldn't be too hard." I looked around him at the girls as they stared at his back adoringly.

"Not hard at all." He spun around and smiled at them.

"That's what she said."

Eric doubled over laughing, causing everyone to turn in our direction.

"She would never say that. Seriously, you suck at this." His face was red as tears filled his eyes from laughing so hard. It was great to see him so carefree. It was a rare occasion, and I knew it was a big deal. Eric pulled me in for a hug, and I tensed, not used to him being affectionate with me or anyone, for that matter. I hugged him back as I glanced over at Tucker, his jaw clenched and his brow furrowed as he watched us. I pulled back, not sure if he was upset.

I smiled at Eric as he shook his head and made his way back to the scantily clad women. His arms were stretched out to his sides.

"Who wants to find out how hard a drummer can bang?"

The girls giggled, and I shook my head, laughing and glancing back to Tucker, but he wasn't there. I scanned the area and found him mounting the motorcycle. A brunette got on behind him, wrapping her long tanned limbs around his body. My heart rate went into overdrive as I watched her lean in and whisper something in his ear, causing him to laugh as his hand went to hers around his waist. My heart was thudding so loudly in my ears I didn't hear Donna's voice until she repeated herself.

"He looks good out there."

I didn't respond, keeping my eyes locked on my boy-friend.

"You should take a walk, maybe pick up some lunch." Her voice wasn't threatening and didn't have its usual edge to it.

"I'm not hungry," I replied as I wrapped my arms around myself. Tucker spoke to the director as the model's hands continued to roam over him. She looked in my direction as she said something to him, and he glanced our way, nodding and laughing again at something she said. Jealousy coiled in my belly, winding me tighter, and I wanted to explode. *This is his job*, I reminded myself. *But you're the one he chose to have on the back of his bike.*

"Suit yourself." Donna walked back over to Tucker and said a few things, everyone's attention on her. Tucker made a face, and I couldn't tell if he was frustrated or angry. He looked my way as they continued to speak quietly. Donna glanced over her shoulder, smiling. What I wouldn't give to wipe that smirk off her face.

The model climbed off the back of his bike, and my heart began to beat normally again until she walked toward me. I held my breath as she approached, but she continued by and disappeared into the dressing room.

I wiped my damp palms on my jeans and tried to relax. The twins made their way across the room, and I wanted to carry on a conversation with them to put myself at ease, but they barely noticed me as they flirted with the other set of twins. I felt completely out of place, wishing I had a pen and paper so I could process some of the feelings that were brewing inside of me. I closed my eyes and began to count down from ten.

"You all right?" Eric asked, and I opened my eyes to see him beside me, his hands shoved in his jean pockets.

"Yeah." I faked a smile, and he cocked his head.

"You expect me to believe that?" He leaned back against the wall beside me. I wanted to open up to him like he had with me, but I was concerned with the way Tucker had looked at me when we'd hugged. Suddenly I felt like I needed to close myself off to him.

"I'm fine." I shrugged as I stared off across the room.

"How did things go with your dad? That must have been crazy." He shook his head.

The girl who had been on the back of the bike moments before walked back by us wearing nothing but a crisp white sheet around her body. I couldn't breathe as I stood up straighter trying to see through the bodies that milled around Tucker. She slipped between them, and I stood up on my toes to figure out what was happening.

"Crazy," I repeated quietly.

"Tuck and I have our problems, but you know he loves you, right?"

That caught me off guard enough to cause me to look at him, momentarily forgetting my worry.

"I know that." I wasn't sure why he had said it, and suddenly it terrified me.

"I don't know why he insisted on you being here for this. It's only going to torture you." Eric shook his head as he shoved his hands deeper into his pockets.

"You don't want me here?" I could handle Donna not wanting me around, but I thought Eric and I had become friends.

He shook his head and took a deep breath.

"You really want to watch some chick putting her hands all over the guy you love? He knows it's going to hurt you."

"He didn't look very happy about it," I mumbled as I tried to see what was happening, but the extras and set helpers were still blocking my view.

Eric chuckled as he ran his hand over his jaw.

"What? You said yourself he insisted I come. That doesn't sound like a guy excited about having some other woman's hands on him."

Donna stepped to the side, and I had a perfect view of Tucker's face. The nearly naked model was straddling his lap. I gasped as Eric leaned in next to my ear to whisper.

"That's because he shot this scene yesterday. He never intended for you to see it. Donna insisted they reshoot it."

I glanced up at him, his face an inch from mine as his eyes locked onto mine.

"He didn't know." Eric's words rang loudly in my ears.

Pain ripped through my chest like someone had actually

stabbed me and twisted the knife. My hand flew up to my heart and landed on the locket Tucker had given me as tears filled my eyes.

The director shouted out a command, but all I could hear was the harsh rapid pounding of my heart in my ears.

I looked up at Tucker as the music began to play. The sheet sagged low on the woman's back, revealing bare skin. Tucker gripped the handle of the bike with one hand, his other roaming over her flesh as he sang into her ear.

My heart is full and my door's always open
You can come anytime you want

I felt my knees grow weak. It was a song he had often sung to me, and my knees began to give out from under me.

I wasn't cut out for this. And suddenly I felt that all-too-familiar feeling, that heavy urgent need to flee. Eric slipped his arm around my waist and held me up against his side, his fingers lightly rubbing over my hip.

"Don't run. These girls can smell fear like sharks. If you leave, they will see it as an invitation to go in for the kill."

"I don't think I can watch this."

"It's all a show. I know he thinks I hate him, and sometimes I do." He chuckled softly. "But I consider you a friend. Tucker wouldn't hurt you."

I sighed, leaning over to give Eric a hug as Tucker glanced at us. I gave him a weak smile, but he didn't return it.

"I think he regrets me being here now."

"He just doesn't want you to be upset. He didn't expect this today. It was supposed to be band shots. I told Donna to call him to let him know, and she said she would." Our eyes met, and we both let out a laugh.

"Well, I think I know why that call was never made."

I was staring at Eric, letting my jealousy start to melt away when I was yanked away harshly, tripping over my own feet and falling back on the hard concrete floor. It took a moment for me to realize what had happened. Tucker's fist swung at Eric as he wrapped his arms around Tucker's waist, pulling him down to the ground. I felt myself scream, the sound coming out ear-piercingly loud.

"Why the fuck are you touching my girl?" Tucker yelled as he gained the upper hand and swung at Eric.

"Shit man, we're friends!" Eric yelled back as he shoved against Tucker's chest.

"She is nothing to you." Another blow from Tucker hit Eric in the mouth, causing his head to bounce off the concrete floor with a loud thud. The twins grabbed Tucker by his arms, yanking him hard off Eric who pushed to his feet and charged Tucker. I screamed again, and he stopped dead in his tracks. Both the men's chests were heaving as they struggled to regain composure.

"I want you out," Tucker yelled.

"I was just leaving." Eric spit blood from his mouth at

Tucker's feet as he shoved by him and walked past me without looking at me.

"Out of the band!" Tucker's shout froze Eric in his tracks. He spun around, glaring back at my boyfriend as I sat frozen between them. The room was completely silent apart from the sound of Tucker's rough breathing.

"You don't mean that," Eric said, no longer shouting, and I could see the hurt in his eyes.

"I do."

Eric glanced down at me, and I knew he was ready to lose it. He had nowhere else to go, and no matter how he had acted in the past, this band was his family. His eyes widened as he realized I had been knocked down during the scuffle, and his gaze turned murderous.

Tucker watched and laughed sardonically as he pulled out of Chris's and Terry's grip, equally pissed off, and I couldn't fathom why.

"She can go with you." He turned and stalked off to the dressing-room door, slamming it, causing the sound to echo throughout the cavernous space. I looked at all of the people who stood around me, sadness in some eyes and satisfaction in others. Tears blurred my vision, and I felt the heavy sobs begging to rip from my chest.

Eric sank down next to me.

"Are you hurt?" he asked, and I shook my head no, but it was a lie. Physically I was fine, but my heart had been stomped and ripped from my chest. I felt like I was dying, and I wished someone would put me out of my misery. He held out his hand to me, softness in his eyes. "Come on."

I slipped my hand in his, letting him pull me from the ground as I groaned. My tailbone throbbed, and I knew my lower back would be bruised. Eric led me toward the exit.

"Don't look back," he whispered, and I nodded, not having any intention of looking at any of those people. I fought the urge to run, but I wasn't even sure I could with the pain in my back.

As we stepped out into the warm night air, the first sob ripped through me. Eric squeezed my hand tighter and continued to pull me away from the building.

"Not here."

I let him guide me as my mind swirled. Tucker was mad at me? I was the one watching my boyfriend practically have sex on top of a motorcycle. Eric had only tried to comfort me and reassure me that Tucker loved me.

"I don't know what just happened."

"I do. I'm sorry, Cass. This is my fault. I never should have even gone over there. . . ."

"No." I stopped, pulling my hand free from his. "I can talk to whomever I want. He should trust me."

"It's not you he doesn't trust." Eric laughed sadly.

"You never did anything to him. You don't deserve to be treated like an enemy."

Eric scratched the back of his head as he stared down at his shoes.

"I deserve it." Sadness marred his voice.

I rolled my eyes, hating that he was slipping back into his anger and depression.

"No, you don't. So you're kind of an asshole sometimes. What he just did was no better than anything you've done."

Eric laughed and shook his head as his eyes met mine.

"Of course you wouldn't know."

"Know what?"

"Tucker and I have a complicated past."

"Define 'complicated,' because my past is as complicated as they come."

"Not here." He glanced around the parking lot before spotting something off in the distance. "Come on." He grabbed my hand again and pulled me across the expansive maze of parking lots.

My legs were quaking, and my back was throbbing as we reached a little dive bar called Corner Pocket. I followed Eric inside as my mind raced, wondering what he was going to tell me. He wasn't the type to open up, so I knew whatever it was, it was a big step for him.

He didn't say anything as he scanned the tiny bar. He walked up to the counter and ordered us two shots of Jack Daniel's and a Coke for me. I waited as the bartender filled his order, and I looked around at the smattering of patrons. I noticed a jukebox off in the corner on the other side of the bar and rounded it to see what kind of music they had. I wanted to listen to something sad, something that reflected the way I felt inside. Hollow, hurting.

Suddenly I felt so lost. I had no idea what was going on with my life anymore. Everything seemed to have fallen into place a few days ago, and just that quickly it had all disappeared out from under me. It was my biggest fear. After my father left when I was younger, I was always afraid of being alone. That was one of the reasons I couldn't leave Jax. Anything felt better than being alone. And now I was facing that reality once again.

"Here." I jumped as Eric's hot breath blew over the back of my neck, startling me. He reached around me holding a shot glass.

I took it and let the liquid burn fire down my throat. He handed me the soda with a smirk, and I slurped it down, grateful he had gotten me a chaser. I wiped the back of my hand over my lips as I took in a deep breath.

"You *almost* drink like a rock star." He laughed, but his eyes were sad.

"You wanted to talk?" I asked as I looked over the tables.

"You want some music?" He dug in his pockets and pulled out quarters. "I asked the bartender for change."

"Thanks." I smiled back, even though happiness was the last emotion I felt. I turned back to the jukebox and picked a few old country songs I remembered from childhood. No one did sadness like country crooners.

We made our way to a small table in the corner. Eric folded his hands together and looked down at his fingers, not saying anything. I didn't want to pressure him, knowing he probably felt as bad as I did after being kicked out of the band.

"He didn't mean it," I said, hoping I didn't need to elaborate and speak Tucker's name.

"Yeah, he did." Eric looked up, his eyes reflecting the pain in mine. The warmth of the alcohol began to warm my body, and I relaxed in my seat.

"I don't care about me, but you getting hurt is crossing a line."

"I'm used to it." I knew how bad that sounded, and I wished I could take it back.

"I know he didn't mean to knock you down." His jaw clenched. "But he did, and he deserves to get his ass kicked for it."

"Please, no more fighting." I knew Tucker hadn't meant for me to fall—that wasn't what upset me. Eric nodded, understanding my need to let it settle.

"When I was in high school, I loved life." He smirked at the memory. He held up two fingers and the bartender nodded at him. "I need another drink for this."

"Did you all go to high school together?" I asked as the

bartender set two shot glasses full of amber liquid in front of us.

"No." He took his shot and drank it back, not even grimacing at its harsh taste. I did the same, but my lips puckered, and I took another drink from my soda.

"I went to Radley High, home of the Rockets. I was on the football team and everything."

"I can't picture that."

He laughed.

"A lot has changed since then."

I nodded, waiting for him to continue.

"I had the perfect life, the perfect girlfriend. She was . . ." He didn't finish his thought.

"What happened?"

"She moved. Broke my heart. First love is a bitch, but we stayed in contact. I loved her. I couldn't let her go. She was my whole world."

"That must have been hard."

"I would have done anything for her." He smiled, his eyes glazing over as he held up his fingers again to the bartender. "We only lived twenty minutes away from each other, but when you aren't old enough to drive, it might as well be a million miles. Living in different school districts made it worse. We tried to see each other on the weekends whenever we could. Eventually our parents got sick of driving us. My mom tried to tell me it was a good thing. I could focus on my future." He shook his head and leaned on the table. "She *was* my fucking future." The bartender sat down our drinks, and Eric took his like it was water.

I swallowed hard, preparing myself to down the drink.

"Don't think about it. Just do it."

I did, and the shot went easily down now that I was beginning to feel the effects of the others. Unfortunately, being intoxicated only magnified the sadness in my gut. I didn't want to think about Tucker.

"You drifted apart?"

"Nah, absence makes the heart grow fonder. I called her constantly, I wrote her songs."

"You had it bad." We both laughed as the song switched and a new one began to play. Eric listened as the singer began to tell of her own heartbreak.

"When my brother died . . ." His jaw muscles jumped under his skin, and I knew it was hurting him to talk about it. My eyes lingered on his swollen busted lip. Regardless of their issues, I knew Eric saw Tucker and the others as his brothers . . . and he had just lost them as well. "I went crazy. I wouldn't talk to anyone. I only wanted her. I stole my mother's car. I had my permit at the time, even though I was seventeen. That's another story."

"I still don't have my license," I confessed, and Eric let out a guttural laugh. I smiled, letting the alcohol sway my mood.

"Why the hell not?"

"I never had a car." I shrugged. "Tucker doesn't really have time to teach me. Not that I could drive that stupid bike."

He laughed, but I stared down at my soda, hoping I could keep from crying.

"I can teach you," he said, his tone level and serious.

"Thanks . . . but you don't have a car either."

"Technicality. You need to learn to drive. You need to be independent."

"Huh . . . I never really thought about it. So when did you get your license?"

He frowned and adjusted in his seat.

"I didn't."

It was my turn to laugh.

"Keep it down. You're going to ruin my street cred." He rolled his eyes. I signaled to the bartender, and Eric cocked his eyebrow at me.

"You're not the only one who wants to numb the pain." I shrugged and took a sip of my soda.

"Right." He paused, and I looked at him expectantly, waiting for him to continue. "That night"—he swallowed hard as he struggled not to let the emotions of that time take over—"I stole my mom's car. Shit, that sounds bad. I drove to my girlfriend's house and she wasn't home. That was normal. Her mother seemed shocked to see me, though. It was odd. I always loved her mother, and we were close when they lived down the road from me. That day, something was different." He shook his head. "It was probably all in my head—I was pretty fucked up about what had happened. So I tried her cell phone and after three tries, she finally answered. She told me she was doing her homework while her mom cooked dinner."

"Oh, no," I said as I realized she had lied to him on the worst day of his life. I closed my eyes as if preparing for a physical blow. I didn't want to see his heart break in his eyes as he told the rest of the story. His warm hand slid over mine, and I opened my eyes.

"It's fine. It was a long time ago." He sat back, his hand sliding off mine. We picked up our shots that had been dropped off while he was talking.

"To friends." He held out his shot glass, and I bumped mine against his, causing some of the alcohol to splash over our fingers. We drank it down as a hard-rock song came on the jukebox. We both glanced over in that direction as another patron rounded the bar and took a seat on his stool.

"Enough of that sappy shit. I drink to forget, not remember."

Eric and I just looked at each other and laughed. I took a drink of my soda and looked up at Eric, waiting for him to continue.

He gripped the back of his neck in his hand as he rolled his head from side to side. His eye was purpling and I could only imagine the lump that was forming from his head slamming the floor. As much as I loved Tucker, in that moment all I saw was Jax, and it terrified me.

"You okay?"

"One of my headaches. It's no big deal."

"Why do you get them?"

"That's another story. We still haven't finished this one. So, as I sat outside of her house in my mother's old station wagon, knowing damn well she wasn't inside, my sadness was replaced with anger. I drove around town checking out all the local hangouts. I knew she had mentioned her friend getting a brand-new Jetta, so I kept an eye out. I saw a candy-apple red Jetta parked outside of Tommy's Pizza. I walked up to the front of the building and I wasn't even mad that she had lied. Shit, I lied sometimes, too. We were kids, but I really needed her." He swallowed hard and cleared his throat. "As I walked in front of the large window in the front of the building I saw her inside with some guy kissing his way down her neck."

"I'm so sorry." My hand flew over my mouth.

"Not as sorry as she was. I grabbed one of those stupid decorative bricks from the little garden under the window and threw it as hard as I could. As soon as it left my fingers I knew I had fucked up. I cried as I drove out of there as fast as possible, like I could somehow turn back time. I wasn't that great of a driver, though, and I didn't see a stop sign. I wrecked . . . hard. I didn't hit anyone else, luckily, but I had a pretty severe concussion and spent a few weeks in the hospital." He looked up at the ceiling before looking back at me. "I lost my brother, I lost my girl, I couldn't get my license. I got put on probation for the window and driving without a license, Coach kicked me off the team. My parents were pissed. They didn't know how to deal with my brother's death, and I became the perfect scapegoat, the ideal punching bag. The rest is rock-and-roll history."

"Geez. That's why you have the headaches?"

"No. Like I said, another story."

I shook my head as I sat back in my seat. "But, what does that have to do with Tucker?"

"I gave up on football, of course, after I was kicked off the team. I began to play my drums more and more. It was a good release for anger, and I wasn't allowed to leave my house. My parents couldn't wait for me to turn eighteen. They wanted me out of the fucking house so bad." He signaled the bartender, and my stomach churned.

"I can't."

"Two beers," he called out and ran his hand over his head. "So, long story just a little longer." He smirked. "I auditioned for Damaged. It was a cool group of guys, and I felt like I finally belonged somewhere, ya know?"

I did know. The band had become my family, and now they had been taken away from me just as they had from him. We fell silent for a moment.

"It was amazing to have people who understood you. I loved it. I gave everything to the band. But one day, *she* walked back into my life."

I was sitting on the edge of my chair now, completely lost

in his sad story and wondering how it had anything to do with Tucker.

"We played a gig at this stupid little dive bar. Kind of like this place." The bartender raised an eyebrow as he sat down our bottles and Eric chuckled. "When she walked in, I couldn't play. I couldn't move. I hadn't stopped loving her. I mean, I hated her, but my heart just wouldn't let go. When our set ended I was dying. It felt like my heart hadn't beat since I last saw her that day when she caused it to stop. I waited for the other guys to get off the stage, and as I went to walk down the steps, I watched Tucker wrap his arms around Cadence and kiss her."

I felt the color drain from my face as I heard her name. I knew Cadence all too well. She had tried her best to break Tucker and me up the night I had found out I was pregnant.

"Tucker stole your girlfriend?"

Eric took a long swig of his beer and set the bottle on the table, spinning it in his fingers.

"Nope. He didn't know. She had lied to him just as she lied to me. I had no idea it was him in that pizza shop until he told me how long they had been together. She never mentioned it. She acted like we didn't know each other. That hurt more than the cheating, I think."

I took a drink from my beer, hoping I could make myself numb enough not to care about Tucker with someone else. My memory flashed to him on the bike with that bitch straddling his lap.

"For the most part I was able to pretend it wasn't killing me inside, but then one day . . ." He shook his head and closed his eyes. I was worried about his headaches, but I didn't want to interrupt him. "She decided to come on tour with us. It was so hard watching them together and knowing she was sleeping so close by . . . with *him*. I knew it wasn't his fault, but it still ripped me apart. He had been like a brother to me."

I reached across the table and slid my hand over his, trying to give him the same comfort as he had given me. His fingers wrapped around mine and he stared down at them and smiled.

"It feels good to be able to talk about this." His fingers unwrapped from mine, and I pulled my hand back, placing it on my bottle.

"Is that why you fight him so much?"

He scrubbed his hands over his face, trying to shake the darker mood that had settled over him.

"No. Cadence had been using drugs here and there. I caught her snorting something one night, and I tried to tell Tucker about it. He flipped out on me, saying I was jealous of him, and he saw the way I looked at his girl. *His* girl. He didn't want to believe she was doing all this crazy shit. One day my pills went missing and I flipped out. My head was killing me. I tried to tell him it was her, but he didn't believe me. Not until one day when we found her in a bathroom after a show. She was lying in a heap on the floor, covered in sweat. I thought she was dead."

"You blame Tucker for what she did?"

"I blame her for her actions . . . but she was a junkie and needed help. He refused to see it. He blamed me, saying I gave her the pills and I was trying to screw up what he had."

"That doesn't sound like Tucker," I said in barely a whisper as I took another drink.

"He got the girl and he let her nearly die. After she finally got the help she needed, he tossed her aside."

"And you wouldn't have? She was *toxic*." I remembered everything that Tucker had told me about her, trying to find a way to defend him, explain his heartlessness.

"I would have walked through hell and back for her."

"You can only take so much before you get burned."

Eric's eyes met mine as he thought over what I said.

"Yeah, I suppose you're right." He took a drink. "I think he is still trying to make it up to himself."

"How so?"

"He didn't let you die."

Suddenly I wondered if Tucker had saved me because he thought it would make up for what happened in the past.

"I didn't mean it like that, Cass. I just meant he wouldn't let someone he cared about get hurt again."

I nodded, but the tears were forming in my eyes and I just wanted to break down.

"Does he know now that you had dated her?"

"Yeah. We got in a fight once and I let it slip. It didn't make things any better between us."

"Obviously," I joked as I looked over his fat lip and bruised eye. He laughed. "I need to use the bathroom."

Eric's eyes scanned the room and he pointed to the back left corner with the neck of his bottle. I pushed from the table and walked on wobbly legs to the door. I hadn't realized how much I had drunk until I stood. The bathroom was a single stall, and I was grateful for a little privacy. I splashed some cold water on my face. This was a lot to absorb. And suddenly, I questioned Tucker's motives for wanting to help me. For the first time in a long time, I felt like a charity case. It made me sick.

I left the bathroom and pulled a one-dollar bill from my back pocket. Eric was staring down at his bottle, lost in memories.

"Can I get change?" I asked the bartender. He took the bill and gave me my quarters. I scanned over the machine, trying to find something to cheer up Eric before he noticed I was out of the bathroom. I flipped through the pages of CDs, reading over the titles carefully. Finally, I found a song I thought might make him smile. I made my way back to my seat hoping to lighten the mood.

As *House of the Rising Sun* began to play, Eric looked up at me and grinned.

"A girl after my own heart." He put his hand on his chest and fell against the back of his chair.

"Did you drink more while I was gone?"

He held up his fingers to let me know he had a little more.

"I think you need to be cut off."

He gave me a frightened looked and I laughed, loudly.

"Not Bobbit style. You need to slow down on the alcohol."

"You might be right." He picked up his bottle and drained the rest of the contents. "But we don't have anywhere else to be."

My heart sank again. I didn't have anywhere to go, and all of my things were on the bus except for my bag from my trip. It was still on Tucker's motorcycle and I wasn't ready to face him yet. I was completely lost. I thought about calling my dad, but he had enough mouths to feed, and not nearly enough food to go around.

"I suppose you're right." I grabbed my bottle and drank the rest of the warming bubbly liquid.

"Tell me about the headaches."

Eric sighed as he recalled the beating from his father two months after the death of his brother.

We sat for several more hours, drinking and reliving our pasts until we both were having trouble walking on our own. We left the bar and stumbled across the expansive parking lot, but everyone was long gone, including Tucker's bike. Sadness consumed me again as I stared at the empty spot where it had been.

"We need a cab," Eric slurred as he looked around.

"I need to call Tucker." I held up the phone for Eric to see.

"You sure that's a good idea?"

"What else are we going to do? I don't have a choice."

He nodded, rubbing the side of his head.

"You need your medicine, and we can't just sleep out here in a parking lot."

I pulled out my phone, expecting a screen filled with missed calls and texts from Tucker. My heart sank when I was greeted by a blank screen.

"Let me call Donna." Eric grabbed his phone and dialed her number before I could argue. I hated Donna. I'd rather sleep with wild dogs than ask her for help, but Eric couldn't go on suffering.

"Where are you?" he asked. Still massaging his head, his eyes closed as he listened. I chewed nervously on my lip, wishing I could make this whole day disappear.

Eric's gaze met mine. I furrowed my brow, wishing I could hear the conversation.

"Why wait for things to cool down? It will only get worse when I come back. This shit needs to be settled."

He fell silent again, and he shifted his weight from foot to foot.

"You know this is bullshit." His entire tone changed, and I knew he was no longer talking to Donna. I wrapped my arms around myself and looked around the parking lot trying not to focus on the bitter fight I had caused. "Fine."

He hung up the phone and began pacing.

"What did he say?"

"He will be here to pick you up in a few minutes."

"What about you?"

"What about me?"

I took a step toward him and he turned around, trying to hide the sadness that was written all over his face.

"He can't just leave you out here."

"Cass, just go with him and fix this for yourself. I'll be fine. He needs you."

"I think I need him more than he needs me."

Eric turned back around, shaking his head as we heard the distant growl of Tucker's bike.

"You guys have been through a lot and that can either make you closer or rip you apart. You have to decide which way you want to go and stick with it."

"That was deep." I laughed, trying to lighten the situation.

"That's what she said." He winked as he smiled. His expression faded as Tucker pulled up beside us. He grabbed the spare helmet from the back of his bike and held it out to me. I looked from him to Eric, hating that he was being left behind. He had been through enough of that in his life.

I walked over to Tucker, my legs shaking from nervousness and inebriation.

"I'm not going to leave him out here." I watched Tucker's expression change to anger, and I held up a hand to stop him before he said something he would regret. I took another step closer and leaned in, kissing him softly on the lips. "I wouldn't ever cheat on you, Tucker, and Eric would never hurt you like that. He is my friend, and he is yours, too. We are supposed to be a family. Family doesn't do this."

"You're drunk," was all he said. Tucker looked from Eric to me several times before he mumbled a curse word and pulled out his phone. He called Donna and told her to come pick up Eric. We all fell silent after he ended the call.

"Just go. I'll be fine." Eric waved his hand at us.

"She'll be here any minute," Tucker replied, not looking at him.

I nodded reluctantly and slid my leg over the back of Tucker's bike. I took the helmet from his hand and secured it on my head. As we circled past Eric I gave him a smile before we took off fast across the deserted parking lot. I held on to Tucker, thankful I could wrap my arms around him again. I was hurt and confused, but Eric's words had struck a chord. We needed to make a choice. We needed to decide if we would let our past pull us apart or help hold us together.

The ride back to the bus went entirely too fast. I didn't want to let go of Tucker, not knowing if things were going to be okay between us. We had a lot to discuss. As the bus came into view I suddenly felt a new wave of emotion. Embarrassment. Luckily, the alcohol made me feel brave enough to pull myself from Tucker. I took off my helmet as he got off the bike, shaking out my hair. Tucker stood beside me not saying a word. He took my helmet from me, looking it over before tossing it on the back of his bike.

"We need to talk." I wanted to clear the air and make all of this go away. I wanted to be mad at him and know that just because I was upset, he wasn't going to leave me. He nodded, rubbing his hand over his hair as he sighed. It might be too late.

He grabbed my hand and began walking by the bus. I trailed behind him, trying to figure out how we would fix this.

"Thank you for helping Eric."

He turned his head to look at me, his eyes narrowed.

"I only helped him so you would get on the bike. I could care less where he goes."

I stopped, pulling Tucker to a halt.

"Why are you acting like this? Eric is your friend."

"You don't know the whole story."

"I know more than you think."

"You know his side."

"That's because you don't tell me anything! Tucker, you know every pathetic detail of my life, and I barely know anything about your past."

"Because it's the past and that's where it should stay."

I pulled my hand from his and crossed my arms over my chest.

"Those who don't learn from history are doomed to repeat it."

"What does that mean?"

The last thing I wanted to discuss was his ex-girlfriend, but I needed to know I wouldn't be kicked aside the first time I screwed up somehow.

"What happened back there was an innocent hug. Nothing more than that. You need to trust me, and you need to trust your friends."

"Eric is far from innocent." He laughed humorlessly.

"What about you?"

"What about me?" he shot back.

"That girl. She was all over you, Tucker, and I didn't see you pushing her away."

"It was for work," he yelled. I glanced behind us, hoping no one from the bus could hear us arguing.

"Why didn't you want me to be there for that then if it was so innocent?" My anger was matching his.

"Because I didn't want it to hurt you. It killed me to see the look in your eyes when you saw us on that fucking bike, sweetheart."

"You got over that pretty quickly."

"I snapped. Eric and I have a very rough history. I didn't mean for you to get in the middle of it."

"I noticed that when I got knocked out of the way." I glared at him. His expression softened, and I could see his eyes tear over.

"I will never forgive myself . . ." His words cut as he struggled to keep his composure. "I didn't tell you to leave because I was angry at you. I wanted you to leave because I had fucked up. I don't deserve you. Not after tonight."

"What happened in there was an accident. Trust me, I know the difference." I took a step toward him and let my arms fall to my sides. He looked up at me, his expression pained.

"It doesn't matter." He shook his head as a tear slid down his cheek. I reached out to wipe it away, but he pulled back, not letting me touch him. "You don't deserve any of this." He kicked at the loose gravel under our feet.

A pair of headlights flashed across us, and we both turned to see Donna pull up beside the bus. Tucker shoved his hands into his jean pockets.

"What are you saying? You are giving up on us just because it got hard? It can't always be perfect, Tucker."

"It won't ever be perfect, Cass. I'm so afraid someone else is going to hurt you that I end up hurting you myself. The way you looked at me after I fought with Eric . . ."

"If you would just talk to him." I sighed, tossing my hands in the air.

"He doesn't have a choice," Eric called out from behind me, startling me with his close proximity. I spun around to see him just a few feet from us, his eyes locked on Tucker.

"I have nothing to say to you, and this is between me and Cass."

"Seemed like it had something to do with me at the studio." Eric walked up beside me.

"You mean when you were whispering in my girl's ear, pulling her snug against your body?"

"He was telling me not to be upset. He told me to trust you, Tucker." I wanted to fix things in my relationship, but first Eric and Tucker needed to mend their relationship. I hated seeing them hurt each other. Tucker looked over at Eric, not sure he believed me. Eric nodded, raising an eyebrow over his bruised eye.

"That doesn't make sense. He has been against me from day one."

"You're my brother, Tucker. Cadence was a life lesson. This band has been the only family I have, and Cass is a part of that now."

"You expect me to believe that after what happened?"

"What happened?" Eric threw his arms out at his sides. "I was cheated on by my girlfriend and later I found out it was with someone I had come to consider one of my best friends. I know you had no clue, Tuck, but it didn't hurt any less."

"You gave her pills and she nearly overdosed!" Tucker was in Eric's face, but he stood his ground. Eric sighed, trying to keep himself calm.

"I loved her. I wouldn't have done anything to hurt her. Just like I wouldn't do anything to hurt you. And I can't let you hurt Cass."

Tucker relaxed, his shoulders sagging, and I knew he finally believed Eric. I reached out slowly and looped my fingers in Tucker's. He looked up at me, his blue eyes red with sadness.

"I know how hard it is to trust people, Tucker. Everyone I ever cared about hurt me in one way or another. I know it is hard for you, too, but we won't ever make it if we don't try."

He nodded, pulling me roughly into his arms. He squeezed me so tightly I could barely breathe, but I didn't care. I wrapped my arms around him and held on to him as his body shook softy and we both cried. Taking such a leap of faith wasn't easy for either of us.

I don't know how long we stood there, holding each other, but when we finally pulled away, Eric was gone.

"You should talk to him . . . alone," I said, taking a few steps back. Tucker nodded and went toward the bus to find Eric. I let out a sigh and looked up to the millions of stars dotting the sky above me. A few minutes later I heard heavy footsteps on the gravel behind me, and I spun around, not sure who was lurking in the dark.

"You okay?" Sarah asked. She was wearing sweatpants and a T-shirt, her makeup scrubbed off her face and her hair thrown back into a loose ponytail. You would never have guessed her alter ego was a powerful rock chick.

"I think so." I nodded. "You heard all that?"

"Bits and pieces. It was kind of hard to miss."

I looked back up at the sky and Sarah did the same.

"You're lucky."

"How so?" I asked, not taking my eyes off the sky.

"He wouldn't have been so angry if he wasn't so deeply in love you. He cares and it scares the shit out of him. He would give you up if it was what was best for you."

"I can't imagine how it would be better for me to be without him."

"That's because you love him just as much." I could see the smile on her face in my peripheral vision. "There is a big difference between loving someone and being in love with him, you know."

"What's that?"

"When you love someone you tell them, but when you're in love with someone you show them."

"What part of that fight was us showing each other our love?" I looked over at her and she looked at me.

"For starters, he and Eric have been on a downward spiral since I met them. They were dead set on letting it end in a bloody mess, but they didn't. That was because he loves you."

She motioned across the parking lot to Tucker and Eric giving each other a hug as they put their past behind them. "We all have shit that scares us. For you it's getting hurt by someone you love. Tucker is afraid to trust. I'm scared to be alone. We all have our demons, but if we can get our demons to play nice with someone else's, well, that makes life worth living."

CHAPTER

Seventeen

I STRETCHED AND TUCKER'S arms coiled tighter around my stomach. I smiled, kissing him lightly on his forehead. He grinned as he slowly opened his eyes.

"I love waking up with you in my arms."

"Good, because this could get awkward if you didn't."

He laughed, placing a kiss on the tip of my nose.

"Gross," Eric called from his bunk, and Tucker and I both laughed.

"Good morning, Eric," I called out.

"What's good about it?"

"I'm going to make pancakes." I listened as he slid out of his bunk and made his way into the tiny kitchen. Tucker frowned.

"What's wrong?"

"I didn't want to let go of you yet." He squeezed me again,

and I peppered a trail of kisses up his neck. "Now I refuse to let go of you."

I pushed against his chest to break free from his grip.

"Come on. I'm hungry."

He reluctantly let his arms go slack and I slid out of the bunk, holding my hand out to him. He took it and stood up with a groan. I glanced down over the rough skin of his knuckles that had been busted and swollen from his fight with Eric. He pulled his hand back and ran it over his hair.

"I'm fine."

I rolled my eyes but walked to the front of the bus to prepare breakfast. I cringed when I saw Eric's face. His lip was not nearly as swollen, and where it had busted open had healed closed, leaving a thin red line. His eye was another story. It had darkened into deep purples and blues.

"You look rough," Tucker called out from behind me as his hands fell onto my hips. I bent over to grab the ready-made batter from the fridge.

"I think it suits me. Chicks dig it."

I shook my head as I listened to them talk as if last night hadn't happened. I was glad that there was no tension in the bus. I had no clue what they talked about, but it seemed that they had worked out most of their problems.

It felt good to cook, even though it was something simple and most of the work was already done for me. I never learned how to cook homemade meals, anyway, so this was the best alternative. I let my mind drift to what it would be like in the future, standing over a stove in my own home. I wondered if Tucker would be around or off with the band traveling the world.

"Smells great," Chris said with a groan as he made his way to the front of the bus. He shoved Eric over so he could sit at the table. Terry followed suit, squeezing in on Tucker's side. Everyone was happy and chatting. I loved days like these; it made everything else worth it.

I stacked the pancakes on a plate, refusing to feed anyone until I had made enough for them to eat at the same time.

After dishing out a stack for everyone, I gave them their plates and leaned back against the counter to eat my own pancakes as I watched them.

"We need this every morning," Terry proclaimed with his mouth full of food.

"I want to try to make beignets." I shoved a bite in my mouth.

"What fancy kind of shit is that?" Eric asked.

"Weird donut things with powdered sugar on them. I had them when I visited my dad. So good."

"Bring some home with you next time," Chris chimed in.

"All right. I'd like to see him again. It didn't feel like we had much time together . . . and I let so much go unsaid. . . ."

I looked up to see Tucker's eyes on me, but I couldn't read his expression. I finished my last bite of food and turned to wash my plate in the sink as Donna came out of her room in the back of the bus.

"I made pancakes." I used my chin to motion to her plate on the counter. She made a disgusted face, turning up her nose.

"Coffee is the only breakfast I need." She squeezed by me and began to make a pot. The bus was so small she had to put her arm against mine to do it, and I wanted to pull away, but I was trying to keep the peace.

"Good to see you all sitting here in one piece. Almost one piece."

Eric laughed at her and I rolled my eyes since my back was to them all.

"I was going to have a meeting over breakfast, but this will do."

"What's up?" Tucker asked. I turned to face the table. Donna glanced at me like she wanted to ask me to go kick rocks, but she didn't say anything.

"The awards show is approaching, and the tour is now heading to the East Coast, as you know. We have several shows along the way, but mostly we will be stopping only to sleep and eat. I need to know you are all committed to making this work. This is a big deal for Damaged and could really propel your careers."

The guys looked around at each other as they all nodded.

"What happened yesterday can't happen again." She glanced over at me, and I wanted to scream that it hadn't been my fault, but that was a can of worms we didn't need to reopen. Instead, I pulled my lower lip between my teeth and kept my mouth shut.

She glanced down at her watch to check the time.

"If you want to get out and stretch, do so now. We will be driving through the day today. Limited stops because of time constraints."

The guys groaned at the thought of being locked in the bus all day, and I couldn't blame them. It was hard enough getting them all to get along, but locking them in together was asking for trouble.

They stood from their seats and began to talk about the upcoming shows. I grabbed their plates and began to wash them, also wanting to be able to get off the bus for a few minutes before we were on the road again. Tucker kissed me on the cheek and headed for the door.

"If you give me a second, I'll come with you." I used the back of my soapy hand to brush my hair from my face. He held up his cell phone.

"I'm just gonna call Dorris and see how she is feeling."

I nodded, focusing back on the dishes and not Donna who was still standing next to me. One by one they left the bus, leaving us alone.

"Things like yesterday are going to happen."

"Tucker and Eric worked out their issues. And Tuck and I are fine."

"I meant the shoot. There will be more, and he will always have women hanging all over him. It comes with the territory."

"I am aware of that." I turned to look her in the eye. "But it's between Tucker and me. You manage his band, not my relationship."

I walked around her, not wanting to give her a chance to respond, and headed outside. I held my hand over my eyes to shield them from the sun as I looked for Tucker. He was a few yards away. He glanced over at me as he took his phone from his ear and began walking toward me.

"How is she?" I asked as I got closer to him.

"Good as can be expected." He shrugged but didn't elaborate. "I have an idea."

"Uh-oh." He chuckled at my response.

"Let's ride today. I hardly ever get to use my bike, and I am dying to spend some time alone with you. Maybe we could get a room along the way when the driver stops for sleep." He flung his arm around my neck and pulled me toward him as we walked, kissing the side of my head.

"That sounds like heaven."

"Good. I can't take a full day of those guys and Donna."

I laughed as we stepped inside a small gas station. The rest of the band was inside loading up on candy, and Sarah was hanging on Derek's arm. I immediately searched for Eric, hoping it didn't bother him to see them together. Knowing what I did now and how painful it was for him to watch Cadence with Tucker, this had to be like reliving the past for him.

He was at the back of the store, looking over the beer selection. He glanced over at me as I walked up beside him.

"You all right?"

He nodded, glancing around. Tucker let go of my hand to find some snacks for the road.

"What kind of beer you want?"

"I'm riding on the bike with Tucker."

He made a face, clearly disappointed.

"Only for a few hours, man." Tucker walked up behind us and clapped his hand on Eric's shoulder. "Need some time alone."

"I hear ya." His eyes locked on Sarah while he responded. I took a step to the side to obstruct his view.

"Grab some beer for us for later." I gave him a smile and he returned it.

"Sounds like a plan." He grabbed a large case of Budweiser and kicked the freezer door shut with his foot. "Grab some beer. Party on our bus!" he called out to the twins who both hooted and hollered in response. Sarah turned around at the commotion and smiled at Eric. He looked like a love-sick puppy and I needed to make sure I pulled her aside and let her know just how fragile his heart was. She wasn't the type to hurt someone intentionally, but I wasn't certain she understood how Eric felt. He didn't care about groupies; his eyes were only for her.

"I'll bring some liquor from our bus," Sarah called over to him, and he winked at her. Derek narrowed his eyes and I let out an audible sigh. So much for a drama-free night.

After we had gathered all the junk food and drinks we could carry, we headed back to the bus to load it up. It was already running, and Donna looked livid that we had taken so long.

"Cass and I are taking the bike," he said as we walked by her. I grinned from ear to ear. I wasn't going to let her bring me down.

"You need to practice as much as possible," she called after him, and he stopped.

"We're only riding for a few hours." His tone was clipped, and I could tell she was getting under his skin. I didn't understand why she acted the way she did. If she took off the ridiculous business-type outfits and threw on some jeans, she would fit right in with the rest of us. Maybe that's why she didn't. She wanted to put herself above us and keep herself isolated. A lightbulb went off in my head, and I almost squealed with excitement.

"I have an idea," I whispered into Tucker's ear. We left the bus, and I was dying to fill Tucker in on what I thought was a brilliant plan. He sat on his bike on top of the small trailer that was hooked to the back of the bus and slowly walked the bike backward off it.

"I'm scared to ask." He put his helmet on. He held mine out and I took it, sliding it over my hair.

"You don't need to ask, because I'm going to tell you," I replied playfully as I slid onto the back of his bike and wrapped my arms around him. "I think we need to hook Eric up with Donna."

"What?" he yelled and turned his head to try to look at me.

"She's hot, for an evil bitch." I shrugged. "Sarah and I could give her a makeover and let her have a few drinks with us today."

"That is an awful plan. What if she's an angry drunk? Can you imagine?"

"She and Eric would get along great then." I laughed. "I'm just saying we see what happens. If she gets laid, maybe she will calm down and Eric may finally stop looking at Sarah with those puppy-dog eyes."

"Come again?" Derek called from between our buses. He walked out beside the bike and crossed his arms over his chest.

"Shit," I muttered into the back of Tucker's shirt.

"What's up, Derek?" Tucker asked, nodding to him.

"I thought I heard you say something about Sarah."

"No." He shook his head. "Just talking about the party. You coming?"

"I think Sarah and I are gonna hang out. Finally have a bus to ourselves."

"I don't blame you. See ya down the road." Tucker started the bike, putting an end to the conversation. Derek waved as we pulled off. I squeezed Tucker, giggling at how close that was. It only convinced me more that we needed to get Eric's mind on someone else.

CHAPTER

Eighteen

WE RODE FOR hours and my legs felt like they wouldn't hold me as I slid off the back of Tucker's bike. I groaned as I stretched, my tailbone not liking the ride.

Tucker pulled off his helmet and ran his hand over his messy hair.

"You all right?" He unhooked my helmet and pulled it off my head. I ran my fingers through my hair, wishing I had pulled it up in a ponytail. It was knotted from whipping around in the wind for the past six hours.

"I'll survive."

"Not good enough. You need to live." He pulled me against him and pressed his lips on mine, kissing me hungrily. My body melted against his as his hand slid lower and he grabbed my butt. I pulled back, smacking him playfully on the chest. I loved seeing Tucker happy and carefree. Lately it seemed like every-one was doing nothing but fighting, and for once most of the issues had been resolved.

"Get a room," Eric yelled from behind us, and we both turned to see the two massive buses now blocking the gas station.

"I was hoping that sound was a tractor trailer," Tucker joked.

"I wish we could ride the rest of the way by ourselves, but I don't think my butt can take it. Besides, we have an evil plan to unleash."

Tucker grabbed my hand, raising it to his mouth and kissing the back of it as we started walking toward the buses.

"Only one problem. If you have Sarah come on the bus to help with your makeover, Eric is going to start acting crazy around her. That is if you can even get Donna to agree to let you touch her."

I rolled my eyes, but he was right. I knew I wouldn't be able to get her on Filth's bus. They lived like a bunch of homeless teenagers. Their manager refused to even stay on it with them, and he drives himself to each gig. I'd only seen him a handful of times, and he had never spoken a word to me.

"How was the ride?" Chris asked as we approached the bus. He already reeked of beer.

"Relaxing," I replied and snuggled into Tucker's side. He put his arm around my waist and pulled me tighter against him. That time alone was desperately needed, but it would be nice to spend some time with him where we could actually talk.

"Better load up the bike. Donna is on a warpath and wants to hurry up and get to where we're going." Chris rolled his eyes. I reluctantly pulled away from Tucker so he could go get his bike and load it onto the small trailer. I used the time to run over to Filth's bus so I could talk to Sarah. She was standing outside the door, leaning against the metal side.

"Isn't that hot?" I asked as I approached her. She shrugged but didn't look up at me. She was busy pulling a clump of her hair between her fingers and inspecting the ends.

"What's wrong?" I asked as I walked up beside her and leaned back against the hot metal.

"Boys are dumb."

"What's new?" I replied sarcastically, and she looked over at me and laughed. Derek came from the gas station, and he didn't look happy.

"What's going on?"

"Just stretching," she said with a sigh. "I should go," she replied to me as she rolled her eyes. "He's in a weird mood."

I smiled and said good-bye, but my stomach tied in knots. I hoped he believed Tucker when he said we weren't talking about his girlfriend. I would hate to be the reason they weren't getting along.

I made it on our bus, trying to think of a way to get Donna

to relax. As I stepped inside I could hear her in her bedroom having a heated phone call. She probably thought the bus was still empty. I did my best to be quiet as I grabbed a bottle of water from the fridge. I didn't want to eavesdrop, but I had never heard her mention having any friends or family.

Whoever she was talking to was making her very upset. I didn't wish sadness upon anyone, but this may work to my advantage. It was time to get her out of her funk and maybe get Eric's mind off Sarah. She yanked open the door to her room and as her eyes caught mine, she narrowed them.

"How has riding with the guys been?" I tried my best to make casual conversation with her, but it was harder than I thought it would be. I didn't trust her, and I knew she would give anything to get rid of me.

"Do I need to answer that?" She slipped inside the bathroom but didn't close the door. I assumed she was checking to see if it was noticeable that she had been crying. It was, but that was only because I could see that look a mile away. I saw it most of my life whenever I looked in my own mirror.

"The rest of the day should be fun. You should slip on some jeans or something and relax with us."

She leaned her head out into the hallway and just looked at me like I was crazy for even asking.

"Come on. What fun is it hanging out with rock stars if you don't let your hair down and party with them every once in a while?"

"This is my job, Cass. I'm not here to party. I am here to work."

"You can do both. You have a fun job—take advantage. I know the guys would love it."

"Yeah, right." She snorted.

"You catch more flies with honey than you do with vinegar."

"I'm not trying to catch anything." She leaned out into the hall again. "Especially whatever diseases these guys have."

I laughed, shocked that she had cracked a joke.

"Well, I can't say what is getting passed around with the twins, but Tucker is a good guy." I tapped my bottle against the table. "So is Eric," I called a little louder.

"I doubt that."

I walked back down the hall a few steps so I wouldn't have to speak too loudly.

"Seriously. He had his heart broken, and he has kind of closed himself off to women. I've never seen him touch a groupie."

"Who is missing out on the rock-star experience now?" She raised an eyebrow and I smiled.

"You know, we don't have to be enemies."

She sighed and leaned against the sink.

"I don't want to be your enemy. I want what is best for the band."

"The band should be happy. Tucker and I are happy together."

She pulled her clip from her hair, and the curls cascaded down her back. She ran her fingers through it.

"You two are a powder keg waiting to be ignited. Did you already forget his fight with Eric, or is that just part of the experience, too?" Her attitude turned sour and I was ready to throw my hands up and tell her to fuck herself, but I still wanted to help Eric. Deep down she couldn't be all that bad. Something was causing her to close off, and my guess was a relationship.

"That had nothing to do with the band. That was personal. It happens. We love each other very much, and I am not going anywhere. If you could accept that, maybe we could be friends."

"I have plenty of friends."

"The person who you were yelling at on the phone? Sounds an awful lot like the fights Tucker and I have that you are complaining about."

"That is personal, and it is none of your damn business." She was staring down at me now, towering over me in her heels with her finger dangerously close to my face.

"If we were friends, you and I could talk about it. It may surprise you, but besides being the band-wrecking whore you think I am, I can be a pretty good listener." I took a step closer.

"Oh, I can imagine the advice you have to give me. You

travel the country with your personal rock star, with no real re-
sponsibilities, no cares in the world, just along for the ride. . . ."
She scoffed. "Your life is a joke."

I narrowed my eyes, wanting to hate her, but suddenly I realized that her hatred didn't come from disgust or pity. . . . She
was jealous. It knocked the wind out of me.

"You know, maybe if you spent your time getting to know
me instead of judging me, you may learn we have some things
in common."

The door to the bus opened and Donna slid the bathroom
door closed. Eric stepped on the bus, followed by the twins
with fresh cases of beer in hand as they talked about a muscle
car they had seen in the parking lot.

"Hey, Cass. Welcome to the party," Eric called out when he
saw me. I gave him a smile, but I felt like I'd let him down given
that I didn't make any inroads with Donna. I wasn't good at
making friends. It wasn't until I moved to Savannah that I made
my first real friend, and I had left her behind when I came on
tour with Tucker.

"Let's get it started." I walked toward the front of the bus as
I heard Donna exit the bathroom and retreat into her bedroom.
I sighed, feeling defeated. Tucker stepped onto the bus and held
up an alligator head.

"What is that for?" I asked as I grabbed an unopened beer
from Eric's hand.

"I thought it would look cool mounted on the front of the bus or something."

I rolled my eyes as I cracked open my beer and took a drink.

"No way." Eric grabbed it from Tucker's hands with a grin. "I want to hang it on a chain and wear it as a necklace."

"Don't be stupid." Tucker took back the head and gave Eric a playful shove. The bus lurched forward, and we all grabbed onto whatever we could to keep from falling. "Jesus, Ivan. A little warning next time?" The driver waved his hand as an apology, and Tucker shook his head, laughing.

"Where's Filth?" I asked, expecting at least a few of the members to join us.

"Band meeting or some shit. They will get up with us at the next stop," Eric replied as he grabbed himself a can of beer. He held it over the sink and grabbed a knife from the drawer.

"What is he doing?"

"Being an idiot," Terry answered.

"I want to be an idiot, too." Chris shoved by his brother and grabbed a beer.

Eric punctured the can and held it to his lips as he opened the tab on top. Within seconds the can was drained into his mouth, and he slammed it into the sink. Chris took his place and repeated the process.

"You're next," he said to me, and I shook my head.

"I am not doing that. I'll spill it all over me."

"It's not that hard."

"That's what she said!"

Everyone laughed so loudly I didn't hear Donna approach from behind me. They stopped laughing, and for a second I thought I had grown a third eye.

"I'd like a turn." She was speaking without the hard edge to her voice I was used to. I spun around to see Donna wearing an old pair of faded jeans and a black tank top. Her hair was down, and she instantly looked ten years younger. She could only be in her midtwenties at most.

The guys just stared at her like they didn't know who she was.

"Grab Donna a beer, Eric. I'm after her," I said.

She gave me an appreciative smile, and I returned it, hoping that things were going to get better after all. This was step in the right direction.

Tucker plugged an old iPod into the little radio they picked up at a truck stop along the tour, and we all relaxed, singing along to music from the eighties and nineties. We took turns shotgunning beers, and after a few, we were brave enough to try Chris's beer bong. The hours began to fly by as we all laughed and shared stories. Donna didn't speak very much, but she listened intently, and Eric made an effort to ask her questions, encouraging her to be a part of the conversation. Under his angry exterior, he was a really great guy.

Tucker and I made sure Eric and Donna sat next to each

other whenever we could make it happen. She relaxed as the night wore on, and eventually she was smacking him on the arm when he picked on her and bumping her shoulder against his.

"We should hit a strip club," Chris said as he pulled the tab off his empty beer can and tossed it at Tucker.

"Come on, Chris, we need to stay on schedule," Donna replied with a small laugh as Eric put his hand over her mouth to keep her from saying we shouldn't go.

"You can't go wrong with strippers." Eric shrugged as Donna bit into his finger and pried his hand from her mouth. "Ow! What the fuck!"

She rolled her eyes and got up from the table, heading for the bathroom. Eric leaned forward and tried to whisper, but in his drunken state it was actually louder than his normal voice.

"I had no idea *she* was hiding under all that bitchiness and long skirts."

"I think she likes you," I whispered back and smiled. Tucker picked up his beer and tipped the can toward Eric in agreement before taking a small sip.

"Too bad she's our fucking manager." He shook his head.

Tucker glanced over at me and I knew he was second-guessing my plan. Donna came back out and propped herself against the counter, grabbing another beer from the fridge and sipping it.

"Why don't we find a place to play a few games of pool?" I

suggested, hoping that a bar atmosphere would be enough to make the single guys happy.

"You don't want to play me in pool. I'm practically a professional," Eric said.

Terry laughed out loud and patted Eric hard on the back.

"What? I could kick your ass!" Eric eyed Terry, and I knew he wanted to accept his challenge.

"I don't know how to play," Donna spoke up, but she didn't object.

"That's perfect. Eric can teach you. It would be nice to all hang out somewhere a little less crowded," I suggested. Everyone looked to Donna as if she was in charge of their every move. I sighed and pushed against Tucker so he would let me out from the table.

I made my way to the driver, bracing myself on the back of his seat.

"Take us somewhere with beer and pool tables."

He nodded and gave me a thumbs-up. I patted him on the shoulder and walked to the little kitchen, leaning against the counter next to Donna. She seemed far less intimidating without her high heels.

"Fine." She rolled her eyes. "I need off this death trap anyway. It's making me sick."

"Should we let Filth know? We need to stick together for the next show," Chris said.

Shit. I hadn't thought that far ahead. Nothing good could

come from Eric watching Sarah making out with Derek. Before I could think of a proper excuse to protest, Chris was on his phone and calling up Derek. They talked for a minute before he hung up and nodded, letting us know they had agreed.

I looked at Tucker, and he just shook his head, knowing tonight was a bust. I looked over at Donna who was staring at Eric. Just great. She was finally starting to come around, and now it was going to explode in her face.

We pulled off the highway about fifteen minutes later, the sun sinking behind the trees. I stepped off the bus, and Sarah came bounding over to me, a smile plastered on her face.

"You're in a better mood." I swayed on my feet.

"Derek wants me to marry him!" She covered her mouth to stifle a giggle.

"He *what*?" I didn't mean to sound horrified, but I could not believe the night was turning out this way. Just a few hours ago, she was on the verge of tears thanks to that guy, and now she was ecstatic.

"He didn't propose, like, officially." She rolled her eyes and grabbed my arm, pulling me away from the bus door. I was thankful for that. In my shock I forgot that the guys would be coming out right behind me. "It was crazy. We had a bad night, and I really thought he was going to break it off again. We went into the back of the bus about ten minutes ago. I was preparing for him to tell me it wasn't working, but he told me he loved me and he was sorry for everything. He said he wanted me to be his wife! Can you believe it?"

I really *couldn't* believe it. Sarah seemed so strong and always had sage advice for whatever I was going through, but something was very off about her relationship, and she didn't seem capable of seeing it. But I had to admit to myself that I didn't know Derek very well, and the only thing I was certain of was that right now Sarah was happy, and I should be happy for her.

"Congratulations!" I pulled her in for a hug.

"Thank you! It means a lot to me. You're my best friend, you know that?"

I beamed. I'd never been anyone's best friend before, and the words made me feel warm, loved, appreciated.

"Just don't say anything. We're kind of keeping it to ourselves, you know, until it's official with a ring and all that."

Tucker came up behind me and threw his arm over my shoulders.

"You ready to go have some fun?" he asked.

"Absolutely." I looked behind us at the bands as they stood together and talked. "Let's get this over with."

CHAPTER

Nineteen

HE BAR WAS pretty much empty given that it was a weeknight, and it took me a minute to remember if it was Wednesday or Thursday. Everything ran together when you lived on a bus. There was no real sense of time or urgency. As long as we made it to the next gig, life unfolded naturally.

We claimed the two pool tables in the back of the bar, and Eric went to get change so we could play our games. Derek watched him like a hawk, which is when I realized Sarah was also at the bar, ordering drinks.

"I'm gonna grab some beers," I told Tucker before making my way to the bar. I positioned myself between Eric and Sarah and desperately tried to think of something to say.

"Can you get some quarters for the jukebox? This place is too quiet."

"Yeah, no problem. No more sad country shit, though."

I laughed, trying not to let it sound forced, but I knew Sarah was still waiting on her drinks.

"I think that machine takes bills." He pulled a small wad of money out of his back pocket and handed me a one.

"You want to come help me find some songs? Wouldn't want to play any country shit."

"Sure." He glanced around me at Sarah, but she was busy talking to the bartender. I pushed Eric toward the machine, hoping I could stall him enough for her to get her drinks and go back to Derek.

We stuck with the theme of the night and played eighties rock and a few one-hit wonders from the nineties. It was always more fun when everyone knew the words and could sing along at the tops of their lungs. After we had picked our last song, Eric went to the bar to grab a round of beers, and I hurried over to Tucker to see if I could get a moment alone with him to let him know what was going on.

Filth was engaged in a full-on death match at one of the pool tables, and the twins played at the other while they waited for Eric. Donna stood beside Tucker, watching them as they tried to explain how the game worked.

"Eric is grabbing the drinks. I need to go to the ladies' room," I said to Tucker before turning to Donna. "You mind helping E carry the drinks?"

Donna glanced over at the bar and nodded before making her way over to help him out.

"I have some news," I whispered as I glanced at the table behind us. Derek had just made a shot, and Sarah was wrapping her arms around him, praising his skills.

"Sarah and Derek are engaged," I whispered into his ear, and he pulled back to look me in the eye.

"This is going to end badly," he replied as his eyes went to Eric and Donna who were heading toward us.

I nodded, not knowing how else to stop the train wreck I had put in motion. I prayed silently to whoever was listening that if they let both bands survive the night intact, I would try to not meddle in my friends' relationships. I knew my pleas normally fell on deaf ears after all I had been through in the past, but I needed a miracle.

"I got next," Eric called out as he handed a beer to Tucker and me. "You wanna play?" he asked.

Tucker wrapped his arms around my waist and pulled my back against his chest.

"We're just watching for now. Why don't you play teams? You and Donna can take on the twins."

Eric looked behind him and the twins as they trash-talked each other and then his gaze fell on Donna who stood on the other side of the table watching.

"You think she will have beginner's luck?" he asked, turning back to us and causally sipping his drink.

"It's pretty hard." I shrugged. "You may have to help her."

He smirked, raising an eyebrow as he tipped the neck of

his bottle toward me. I knew exactly what he was thinking.

"That's what she said." I laughed, and Tucker and Eric chuckled.

Sarah yelped from behind us, and we all turned to see what had happened. Derek had pinched her butt hard and she smacked him playfully before pulling him in for a kiss. I looked back at Eric who looked devastated.

"This looks easy enough," Donna said as she walked up beside Eric. His attention shifted, but I knew he was not in the greatest mood. It took very little to set him off.

"We can take them," he replied, his eyes drifting down to her chest for a split second, but I had caught it.

"I need to go to the bathroom." Sarah grabbed my arm and yanked me out of Tucker's embrace. This night was not going to be easy, but I wasn't going down without a fight. I held out my beer to Tucker, and he took it to hold for me. I gave him a pleading look to save me, but he only shrugged and took a drink, ready for the inevitable.

We made our way back to the tiny two-stall bathroom, and I cringed when I saw how disgustingly filthy it was. I've seen poor, and this wasn't it. It was downright lazy.

Sarah primped herself in front of the mirror as I watched, and it didn't take long for her to casually bring up Eric.

"Eric seems like he's in a good mood."

"Yeah. He's having a good time." Anyone with a pulse could spot Sarah and Eric's attraction to each another, but now she'd promised herself to Derek. I knew she thought her flirting was harmless, whereas to Eric it was anything but that.

"What's with Donna tonight? She seems different."

"She's actually making an effort. It's really nice."

"An effort to get laid," she mumbled and dropped the subject, but I could hear the bitterness in her words. "You guys getting rooms after this? I'm dying to sleep in a real bed for once."

Wrapping myself in a fluffy comforter and having room to roll around seemed like heaven.

"I hope so. I'll say something to Tucker."

"Can't wait." She was all smiles as she turned to leave the bathroom. Part of me wanted to stop her and tell her how Eric felt about her, but I let her walk out, following behind her. I couldn't mess up such a happy night for her. I had to trust she knew what was best for her own life. Even if she didn't, it was a lesson in life she was meant to learn.

I tried to plaster a realistic smile on my face as I walked over to the pool tables, but I felt like I was being ripped in two. I wanted to do what was best for both of my friends, but it just no longer felt possible. Someone was going to end up getting hurt.

I was surprised to see Eric leaning over behind Donna and guiding her on her next shot at pool. I smiled at Tucker, and he returned the gesture, holding out his arm for me. I slipped under it, snuggling into his side as we watched them play. I took my beer from Tucker's hand and took a little drink.

"They did two rounds of shots while you were gone," he said quietly into my ear before kissing my earlobe. I closed my eyes, savoring his sweet gesture. Tonight was about living in the moment, and I missed that.

"We should get a room tonight." I looked him in the eye to gauge his response. His eyes fell to my lips, and I could feel the electricity pulse between us. I'd missed this feeling, the thought of him touching me. And suddenly, all I could think about were his hands on my skin. He glanced over at Eric and Donna. They were laughing as she hit the cue ball and it spun and touched nothing.

"I'll talk to them. At least something good can come out of this night." He pulled my face to his and kissed me softly, but there was nothing innocent about the way his lips pressed against mine. I smiled, forgetting all of the chaos that brewed around us. Things between us were right, even when the world was crumbling around us.

Donna yelled and her arms wrapped around Eric. I could tell by the way his hand slid down her back that they were actually connecting. Maybe he wouldn't react too badly to Sarah's news if he really felt like there could be something between him and Donna. . . .

As the night began to wind down and everyone seemed to be losing their spunk, Tucker brought up the idea of getting rooms at a hotel. Donna was apprehensive, but she was outnumbered and conceded fairly easily.

Donna went off to use the ladies' room before we left, and I used the opportunity to talk to Eric and see how the plan was working.

"You and Donna seem pretty cozy," I said.

"She's all right." He finished off the last of his warm beer, making a face at its bitter taste.

"Maybe you guys could room together," I suggested, and he looked over at me, rolling his eyes.

"Is that what all this has been about? You're trying to get me to hook up with her? Why? She's been nothing but mean to you this whole trip."

I shrugged. I had no good reason to help Donna; I'd just hoped it would give us all a chance to become friends. But really I just wanted to see Eric happy. Filth was saying their goodbyes and walking out of the bar. Eric's eyes followed them.

"It would just be good to see the both of you let go and have some fun," I said.

His gaze went back to me, and he nodded once but didn't say anything back.

CHAPTER

Twenty

"THIS IS REALLY nice." I looked around the hotel room. Everything was white, floor to ceiling. The bed was covered in a dozen fluffy pillows, and the lamp next to it was covered in white feathers. "Like stepping inside a cloud."

Tucker walked up behind me and pressed himself against my back as his arms looped around my waist.

"I was thinking this is more like Heaven." He placed a small kiss on my neck. A smile spread across my face, and I couldn't have agreed more with him. We hadn't had a night alone during the entire tour. I turned around in his arms to face him, his hands pressed against my lower back, holding me against him as I placed my hands on his chest.

"I don't know . . ." I had no idea what I was trying to say. I had put off being intimate with Tucker for so long that now I was nervous.

"It's just you and me tonight. We can do whatever you want. We can stay up all night and talk, we can play a game, we can write music. . . . It doesn't matter as long as we're together."

He was right. Nothing else mattered: the past, the fights, and the long road we traveled to get here, literally and figuratively. All that mattered was that he and I were together.

"I love you, Tucker."

"You have no idea how much I love to hear you say those words." The pad of his thumb slid over my lower lip. "I love you so much, Cass."

I pushed my lips against his, not wanting to spend another minute contemplating what would be best and just do what felt right in this moment. I wanted nothing more than to make love to the man I fell in love with. Tucker kicked off his shoes, never breaking our kiss as he held on to my waist and guided me backward toward the bed. I slipped off my shoes, nearly tripping us both, and our lips pulled apart for us to laugh, but he quickly covered my mouth with his again. I grabbed the bottom of his shirt and pulled it up, running my hands over the ridges of his stomach muscles.

He yanked his shirt over his head, not wanting to waste another second. I smiled as the back of my knees made contact with the mattress. I grabbed my shirt and pulled it over my head. His gaze dropped to look over my body before he pressed his warm chest against mine. His fingers slid around my back, finding the closure to my bra. He rolled it between his fingers until it went slack.

His fingertips ran over my shoulders and he dragged them down my arms, leaving goose bumps in their wake as he pulled the straps from my shoulders. I let my bra slide down over my hands and fall to the floor between us.

"You are so beautiful." His fingers tangled in my hair as he pulled my mouth to his, sucking my lower lip.

My hands explored his toned chest as he worked to rid us of the rest of our clothing. He undid the closure of my jeans and shoved them over my hips. I stepped out of them as I ran my nails down his stomach, his muscles flexing beneath my fingertips as his breath caught. I loved that my touch gave him that reaction. I unbuckled his belt and undid his jeans as my tongue tangled with his, and he helped kick his jeans off. We lost our balance and fell back onto the bed. Tucker laughed, brushing my hair from my face as he placed a gentle kiss on my forehead.

"We don't have to do this tonight. I'll wait as long as it takes. We have forever."

I slid my hand in his messy hair and pulled his lips back to mine. The playfulness was quickly replaced with hunger for each other. He wanted to spend forever with me, and I didn't want to waste another second of it second-guessing myself.

He pushed his hips against mine, and I slid my nails down his back until my fingers touched the fabric of his boxers. He pulled back from me and stood at the edge of the bed as he shoved his boxers down and kicked them off. His eyes took in every inch of my body as he leaned over and looped his fingers in the sides of my pale-yellow panties. He slid them down slowly and tossed them aside as he lowered himself back on top of me. He kissed along my jaw and down the length of my neck. I wrapped my arms around him and held his body against mine. His mouth moved to my ear, and he kissed my earlobe.

"I love you," he whispered into my ear as he rocked his hips against me and slowly made love to me.

CHAPTER

Twenty-one

 FTER OUR NIGHT in the hotel, nothing was going to rain on our parade. Not even spending a few more days in a cramped bus. Tucker and I checked out of our room and waited in the lobby for everyone else to join us. The twins arrived first, hungover and moaning like they were on the verge of death.

After a few more minutes of waiting, we had the receptionist call up to Eric's room.

He appeared shortly after, looking like he had been hit by a train.

"Jesus, what the hell did she do to you?" Chris asked.

"Who?" Eric looked around at all of us.

"Donna." Chris laughed.

"She went back to the bus last night. You didn't actually think I was going to sleep with her when she was that drunk, did you? Besides, how awkward would the rest of this trip be?"

That left everyone speechless. We just glanced at each other, impressed that Eric had decided against it.

"Let's get back to the bus so we can get on the road." Tucker stretched as he yawned.

The afternoon sun was blinding, and I couldn't get back to the bus fast enough. I felt like Tucker and I had hit another milestone in our relationship, and I was ready to see what else lay ahead.

We spent the next few hours sleeping as we headed west. The band needed to rehearse later, and Donna had already lined up a place for them to do so. The Video Music Awards were coming up fast, and they needed as much time as possible to make sure everything would be perfect for their biggest show to date.

When we arrived, Donna came out of her room in full bitch mode, with matching outfit. The time out with us had done little to change her demeanor in the light of day—in fact, it seemed to only worsen her mood now that she was clearly nursing a hangover—but it gave us all a little insight into who she was deep down.

I got to work on cleaning up the bus. The sink was still full of empty beer cans, and junk-food wrappers were strewn about. It took me a full hour to get the bus looking semi-decent.

I decided to give my father a call and catch up on how June was doing with the pregnancy.

I dialed my father's number and sat down on the edge of our bunk.

"Hey," he said as he answered the phone.

"Hey. How is the family?" I asked, making small talk.

"Great. June is hanging in there, but no baby yet."

"I can't wait to meet my new brother or sister."

"Any day now." Something was off about his tone, and it was starting to worry me.

"I'd like to fly you guys out to us once the baby is old enough."

"I don't think we will be able to do that, princess. It's not a good time."

"Well, whenever. No set date, just an idea."

"I think you should have a chat with Tucker. We aren't welcome out there."

I couldn't wrap my mind around what he was telling me. "I don't think Tucker would mind you coming out here. What would give you that idea?"

"Just talk to him. I have to go." With that, the phone went dead. Tucker was at practice with the guys and I was forbidden from "distracting" him, as Donna put it, but this was my family and if Tucker had interfered, I needed to know.

I headed toward the old brick building that sat adjacent to the concert hall. I was angry, and I didn't want to blow up on

Tucker without knowing the full story. I pushed open the door, and my eyes landed on Donna who looked pissed off, much like she always did when she saw me.

"Can I help you?"

"Nope. This doesn't concern you." I walked by her, and I could tell she wanted to reach out and stop me, but she didn't. I pushed open the next door and stopped dead in my tracks. Tucker sat on a small couch with guitar in hand next to a brunette, their legs touching, her hair hanging down like a curtain blocking his face. They were laughing but stopped abruptly as I entered. The woman sat back in her seat, looking up at me expectantly like I'd come to deliver them lunch or something.

"Am I interrupting?' I didn't care if I sounded like a bitch. I crossed my arms over my chest and eyed Tucker.

"Of course not." He sat his guitar down beside him, propping it against the arm of the couch. "What's wrong?"

I looked at the brunette who made no movement to leave, and I wanted to scream at her to get the fuck out, but I needed to focus. I'd come here to have a rational conversation with Tucker.

"I just spoke to my father."

Tucker's eyes fell, and I knew immediately he had talked to him. He glanced to the brunette next to him.

"Can we get a moment alone?"

She nodded and got up, walking around me with a polite smile. I closed the door behind her and turned back to Tucker.

"Who the hell is that?"

"She's a vocal coach that Donna found to help me work out this song."

I sighed, pissed that all of my feelings of jealousy from the video shoot came rushing back. I tried to shove them aside as I sank down on the couch beside him and wrung my hands together.

"What did you say to my father?"

"Just let it go, Cass. I did it for your own good."

"Did what? Neither of you has told me anything, and I am getting really tired of being treated like a fragile piece of glass. Spit it out."

He sighed, resting his face in his hands with his elbows propped on his knees.

"I made sure you wouldn't get hurt again."

I didn't respond. I didn't know how to. I needed to know what had happened.

"Your father, if you want to call him that, just wanted money from you."

"That's not true."

"It is, Cass. He called me after your visit. He asked if I could loan him a couple grand to get on his feet. I turned him down and told him my money was tied up with the band right now. He said he knew that couldn't be true, that you had mentioned that the band was doing really well, that I'd paid to fly you out there. He has been texting me nonstop since. I offered him five grand but told him he would have to leave you alone, never contact you again. It was just a test, Cass—I never thought he'd take it. He took the money. He didn't even hesitate."

My heart shattered into a million fragments.

"He had to, Tucker. He has a family. He is struggling to make ends meet."

"No, Cass. He didn't have to take the money. He could have kept right on doing whatever he was doing before he saw you on that magazine. But he didn't. He chose to cut you out of his life for five grand."

I had never felt this rejected. For a brief moment I had a family again, I had siblings. And now . . . they were gone.

"Why would you do this to me?" I knew Tucker wasn't the one to blame, but if he had just left this alone, I would still have them. I preferred blissful ignorance to the harsh reality of life. I'd had enough of that in my past.

"Cass, I didn't want to see you hurt. I was trying to protect you." He reached for my hand, and I pulled back, pushing to my feet.

"But what did you think would happen? Did you think I would thank you for taking my family away from me?"

"I expected your father to turn me down. I expected him to be the man he is supposed to be, one who would never put a price tag on his relationship with his daughter. I was shocked . . . horrified when he accepted." Tucker shook his head. "But the moment he did, I knew he was no good for you.

Toxic. I knew I needed to get him as far away from you as possible. Don't you see, Cass? All he wanted was money from the start. That's why he reached out. . . ."

I shook my head, begging the tears to stay at bay. I didn't want to be the fragile thing he thought I was. I wanted to be strong. I needed to be strong.

"Now that you have proven yourself right, I hope you feel better. I'll let you get back to this private session with whoever that woman is." I turned to leave as his fingers looped around my elbow to stop me.

"Don't do this, sweetheart. I didn't want you to get hurt, but you would have eventually."

I turned back to him, glaring.

"You wanted to make sure you were the one to do it? Congratulations. I'm out of here." I yanked my arm free and shoved open the door, causing it to bounce off the wall behind it. The brunette jumped, startled by the noise. I narrowed my eyes at her as I walked out into the lobby, not bothering to look at Donna.

I'm sure she thought I was being jealous and flipping out about Tucker being alone with whoever that woman was. It didn't matter. She won. She had successfully driven a wedge between Tucker and me, and now he had managed to push me away. I was beyond done and felt more alone than ever.

I had given up everything and tagged along on this tour and somehow lost myself completely in the process. No matter what I tried to do, I couldn't crawl out from under Tucker's enormous shadow.

I stood in the parking lot, not sure which way to turn. I had no one and nowhere to go. I was lost and alone. The door opened behind me and I turned, wanting to run into Tucker's arms, but I came face-to-face with Donna.

"What could you possibly want?"

"I think this relationship has become unhealthy, and I don't think it's good for Tucker."

"Good for Tucker? You have a lot of nerve trying to tell me what is best for him. He is *my* boyfriend. Just in case you didn't notice, I am the one who is getting hurt, not him."

"In any case, this isn't good for his career."

"That's all you care about, isn't it? You could give a shit about whether he is hurting. He's just a dollar sign to you."

She crossed her arms over her chest.

"That is what he hired me for. Don't forget that if he didn't want me here, I wouldn't be here."

She was right. They could easily fire her and find another manager. Tucker was the leader of the band and could make that decision, but he hadn't, even if it was making me miserable. Emptiness settled inside of me and I was ready to run, to escape this feeling. I was in self-destruct mode. I wasn't thinking clearly. I shook my head and walked away from her. I didn't have it in me to fight any longer. I was devastated by my father's ability to choose money over his own child. I felt like he'd abandoned me all over again.

I ran back to the bus and grabbed my purse and a tote bag. I couldn't take it any longer, any of it. I threw in a few of my belongings, not wanting to waste too much time. I didn't want to run into Sarah or Eric or anyone who would try to convince me to stay. I knew I was being irrational, but this time, I wasn't strong enough to fight my instinct to flee.

I tossed my cell phone on the table and left, hoping I wouldn't have to walk too far to find a decent hotel. I needed to find an inexpensive way to get back to Georgia or as far away from anyone I knew here. I could become whomever I wanted to again. I could start over.

I pulled open the door to the bus and came face-to-face with Tucker. He took a step onto the bus, and I took one step backward. His eyes fell to my bag and back to my face.

"You were leaving me?" The pain in his voice sliced through my heart like a hot knife.

"Tucker." My voice shook and I swallowed hard, trying to summon my strength.

"Don't, Cass. You promised." He shook his head. "Do you have any idea what it would do to me to come back here and find you gone? Do you even care?"

Tears began to flow freely down my face, and I wanted to press myself against him and be wrapped in his arms, but I stayed frozen.

"Of course I care, Tucker."

"If you did, you wouldn't do this shit. Not again."

"You shouldn't have called my father."

"I couldn't let him hurt you, Cass," he yelled angrily.

"Instead *you* hurt me."

"That's not true."

"It is true." I raised my voice, refusing to be painted as the bad guy. I needed to stand up for myself. "You've been pulling away from me ever since Donna showed up. You didn't give me credit for my song, and now you're interfering with my family."

"Donna is our manager and I won't always like the things she does, but she is doing what is best for the band. And I said I was sorry about the song, Cass. I . . . I don't know what else to do. . . ." Tucker sighed, then turned and looked me straight in the eye. "And *I* am your family, Cass. Not some asshole who abandoned you when you were little and doesn't give two fucks what happens to you. He should have been there to protect you from Jax, but he wasn't. I was." He was yelling now.

I placed my hands over my face and began to sob, the truth in his words finally sinking in. Tucker was the only one who had ever been there for me, no matter how hard I tried to push him away. His arms wrapped around me as he pulled me tightly against his chest. His cheek rested on top of my head as he co-cooned me. As much as I tried to fight it, from fear of being hurt, he wasn't going to leave me. No amount of jealousy or family drama was going to make him run away. I finally felt safe.

"Don't cry, sweetheart."

His words only made my cry harder as his hands rubbed soothingly over my back.

"I'm sorry I yelled at you," he whispered into my hair and placed a kiss on the top of my head.

"Please don't apologize. This isn't your fault. I'm used to people using me and not caring. It's hard to believe that you really love me sometimes."

His grip tightened around me.

"You didn't need him then, and you don't need him now. We have each other, and I promise you I will never leave you."

"I don't know what I would do if I didn't have you."

"You won't ever have to find out." He pressed his lips against my forehead, and I sighed in relief, finally feeling like I'd made it home.

Epilogue

THE CROWD WAS electrified as the awards show began to kick off. Everyone stood up from their red-velvet-wrapped chairs and cheered. Some people were dressed to the nines in what looked like overdone prom gowns while others kept their rock-and-roll or grunge edge. I dressed in a black skirt with a simple white top that said DAMAGED across the chest. Donna had had them made up to sell at the concerts. The stage was broken down into three sections and curved around the front row of the audience. The lights from the ceiling flickered to the beat of the music, and it was like being at a rock concert times ten.

I'd never seen this many people in one place in my entire life. Everyone who was anyone in the music industry—plus a few lucky fans—was in attendance.

I held on to Sarah's hand as if she was my lifeline as we

sat a few rows back from the main performance stage. It was amazing to see so many famous faces all around us. Most I didn't recognize, but Sarah knew all of their names. She pointed them each out to me and sang a few chords of their most popular songs so I would get excited with her. It was overwhelming to be surrounded by so much talent and success. This was exactly what I wanted for Tucker. He had worked so hard and to see his dreams coming true made my heart swell with pride.

The ceremony seemed to drag on forever as I waited for Damaged to take the stage. I got to hear a lot of bands perform songs that I loved, and we danced and cheered along for all of the award winners. It was surreal. Donna was backstage, and I was relieved that I wouldn't have to put up with her, but I wished I could see Tucker before he took the stage. He insisted I sit in the crowd and enjoy the show. It was a once-in-a-lifetime opportunity, and he didn't want me to miss anything. I wondered who he was meeting backstage and if he had gotten to shake hands with some of the musicians who had influenced his career. As much as Donna and I clashed, I knew he and the rest of the band were in good hands with her. She had taken their career to a level Tucker dreamed of since he was a boy, and after tonight, their star was destined to rise even higher.

There was a brief remembrance for all those in the music business who had passed away this year. They played a video of the stars as sad music played in the background. I teared up as I thought of all those who I had lost, my father included. But at least his reappearance had brought me some closure; I was no longer wondering what had become of him and if he ever tried to contact me. Now I knew, and I could move on with my new family, one that I'd created for myself.

By the time the video stopped, fog started rolling out over the performance stage. Tucker's voice began to sing, and the crowd hushed as he sang a slow love song that I had never heard, and I realized it was a mix of some of the lines I had written interwoven with ones he had added himself. The fog began to clear, and all I could see was Tucker, gripping the microphone in his hand. Sarah and I stood and swayed to the music, his voice haunting as he closed his eyes and sang about losing someone he loved. I knew he was singing about our child, and I wanted to rush the stage and wrap my arms around him.

It was amazing to see him take something so tragic and make it into something beautiful. He continued to sing about his heart being full and finding the love of his life. Even in the darkened room, I'm sure it was obvious I was blushing.

If you give your love to me, I will fly with broken wings
Let me fill these empty sheets, show you how love is supposed
to be

As the last note faded, the crowd erupted in applause and the women screamed.

"Thank you so much. It means a lot to us to get up here and sing for you all, and we appreciated the warm welcome." The crowd grew loud again and he waited to continue speaking. "Life is short, and it is important to tell those we love how much they mean to us every chance we get, so, Cass Daniels, I want you to know that I love you more than life itself. That song was for you."

The sound of the audience was deafening. It almost drowned out the sound of my heart thumping in my ears. I was in shock. Tucker had not only professed his love for me in front of a crowd of thousands but also to everyone who was watching on television. My fingers absentmindedly went to the locket necklace he had given me when we first met.

"I need to see him," I shouted over the crowd to Sarah. She grinned and pulled me out to the aisle. We made our way between the rows toward the back of the room.

"This is the wrong way. The stage is over there." I stopped. She tugged on my arm to encourage me to keep walking.

"They have a back entrance," she said as we slipped through the doors.

"How do you know this?" I asked.

She sighed loudly as she pushed open the next set of doors flanked by security.

"Trust me."

I walked by her and outside the doors, stopping dead in

my tracks as I came face-to-face with Tucker who was surrounded by the rest of the band. There were all sweating and
out of breath, fresh from the stage. They must have run
around the building to reach us.

"What are you doing out here?" I asked as I stepped toward
him. "That song . . . it was incredible. . . ."

"We make beautiful music together, and I don't ever want
to write another song alone." He sunk down on his knee and
my hands flew over my mouth as I gasped. He pulled a chain
from around his neck that had been tucked inside of his T-shirt.
Dangling from the chain was a ring. He took it off and dropped
the ring in the palm of his hand.

"From the moment I met you I had everything I ever
wanted in life. All of this is just a bonus. Without you in my life
the music has no heart, because I gave it to you the moment we
met. Will you marry me?"

I couldn't even speak, I was so overwhelmed with emotion.
All I could do was nod my head as he slipped the ring onto my
finger and stood, wrapping his arms around me and lifting me
from the ground. We had left out of the side exit, but it didn't
take long for the paparazzi to discover something was going on
and flashes went off around us like lightning.

I grabbed his face on either side and pressed my lips against
his and everything else faded into the background. For the first
time, Tucker didn't try to hide our relationship from the world.

Instead, he was flaunting it. Our friends all clapped and cheered, shouting their congratulations.

When I used to try to picture what the future held for me, I could barely see past the trailer park. My only goal was to survive. But now, for the first time, I had a reason to *live*.

Acknowledgments

ALEXANDRA LEWIS: One of the best editors in the business.

Kimberly Whalen: An amazing agent who has helped me through every step of this amazing journey.

Lauren McKenna: For taking a chance on my books. She is not only a great editor but an amazing person.

Simon & Schuster: For helping me live my dream.

I am forever grateful.